Morningside

By Priscilla McDaniel

PublishAmerica
Baltimore

ISBN: 1-4241-3816-7
PUBLISHED BY PUBLISHAMERICA, LLLP
www.publishamerica.com
Baltimore

Printed in the United States of America

Morningside is dedicated to my mother,
Mary Virginia Martinson
July 1916-May 1998

Acknowledgements and Thanks

I would like thank my sister Susan Barnhill-Chandler, Linda Wolfe, Aaron Flores, and Ann Wangberg of Sacramento, California for their proofing and editing help. Also a grateful thank you to my friends in Ventura & Santa Barbara Counties, California for their encouragement and input when I first began writing: Janice, Thea, Sharon, Genny, Rusti and Ron.

For his encouragement I thank my friend and mentor, Andy Flink. His patience in assisting me with the details of my writing endeavors are invaluable.

Words cannot express my gratitude to Edward Chandler of West Sacramento for his generous and distinguished art work in the cover design, Thank You Edward.

Most particularly I wish to thank my devoted husband, Ed, for his patience, support and understanding throughout the long and arduous writing process of Morningside

Thank you Father God, in the name of Jesus, for your blessings, And for giving me the joy of writing.

England—1815

Chapter 1

Veronica Hunter gazed dreamily out the window of the Morningside Inn reflecting on her good fortune—her marriage to Gavin Hunter, a handsome young lord who loved her as much as she did him. Her father was quite pleased with the match, but her mother had been most particularly ecstatic about it. Not because the couple loved each other, indeed not, it was his great wealth of which she was most proud.

"And such a fortune he has my dearest Veronica," Mrs. Stuart had said as she watched her eldest daughter dress that morning for the wedding. "I know you will see to it that through Mr. Hunter's connections Louisa and Harriet will make excellent attachments as well."

"Really, Mother, must you talk about such things on a day like today!" Veronica had admonished. "Colette and I have both made good alliances; between us you need not remind me of my duty to my sisters. I am certain there will be plenty of eligible bachelors for them to choose from when you visit for Twelfth Night."

"Well, just remember," her mother reproved, "love will have nothing to do with the matter. What they need are men of means, as they have little enough of their own."

"You look far away darling," Gavin said, gently kissing Veronica's neck as she stared out the window at a brook lined with willow trees and blossoms. "Is everything all right?"

"Yes, of course, I could not be happier," she answered feeling excitement from the thrill of his touch, at the same time pushing thoughts of her family far away. "I shall never forget this place. It is as if you had the trees and flowers planted just for me."

"Indeed, I did," he teased, caressing her shoulder with his hand. "I did however, order chocolates and a white rose to be placed atop our pillows every night."

"It's like a dream." She turned and gazed up at his black wavy hair, and her brown eyes sparkled beneath long lashes. "I have waited so long for this day, and now I can scarcely believe I'm here. It is more beautiful than I ever imagined."

"When the arrangements were made, I had hoped you would be pleased," he said, standing a full head taller than her, with a trim, masculine build and firmly set chin.

Gavin had reserved the top floor of the picturesque Morningside Inn, located forty miles north of London, England. Known for having the most luxurious lodgings outside of London, the Morningside hosted all mahogany floors and paneling, silky Persian carpets, burgundy velvet draperies, exquisite inlaid gold-framed windowpanes, crystal chandeliers, and porcelain urns filled with white roses. Nearly a fourth of Gavin's household staff had gone ahead, eager to prepare the newlywed suites and fill it to the brim with red and white roses and a myriad of other fragrant June flowers. He had planned for himself and his bride, Veronica Anne, Stuart, Hunter, to spend the first three weeks of their six month honeymoon at the inn.

"Would you like to have dinner served up here for our first night together?" Gavin asked.

"That would be nice, though I cannot say I am very hungry."

Following their late supper they took a stroll through the inn's gardens and enjoyed the sweet fragrance of roses and gardenias. When they returned to their rooms, they relaxed by the soft glow of candlelight and sipped a glass of brandy. After preparing for bed, Veronica sat at her dressing table and brushed her hair, even though her personal maid, Margaret, had already done so.

Enraptured and aroused, Gavin watched his bride and spoke almost in a whisper, "I have wanted the feel of your hair in my hands almost from the first time we met."

He took the brush from her and ran his fingers carefully through her dark tresses, kissing them as they fell. His ocean blue eyes moved freely up and down her hourglass figure, and with controlled desire he traced her cheeks and soft lips with his hand and kissed her neck. Then, as if weightless, he lifted her tenderly in his arms and carried her to their bed, gently touching his mouth to her forehead, her eyes, and the tip of her nose. When their lips met, with hearts pounding and breath ragged with passion, they willingly and fervently surrendered to each other.

During their days at the Morningside Inn, they spent endless quixotic times together playing backgammon, taking walks, enjoying picnics and boating. They dined on magnificent fare of foul, fish, beef and duck, superb desserts of chocolates and crèmes, discriminating wine with supper, and the finest brandy before bed.

The third week in June Gavin and Veronica left the inn for Dover then sailed the English Channel to Calais. In Calais they commissioned a French Barouche, an oversized luxury carriage, for themselves and another smaller black carriage for their servants and overflow of trunks.

"It's wonderful being here with you amidst such peaceful pastures and idyllic scenery," Veronica declared, as they traveled along the coast road to Boulogne before turning inland towards Paris.

"I have felt the same way since our wedding day." He paused and a grin crossed his clean-shaven face. "I've been thinking about our families and I have to admit too that it is utterly blissful to be here with only the two of us. In particular my aunt, Lady Ramsay, comes to mind. During our crossing from Dover, I observed one fastidious woman with her daughter. I think I pointed them out to you."

"Yes, I remember them quite well. I believe I thought the same as you. She was much like Lady Ramsay and her daughter, Lillian, who is never allowed to talk or leave her mother's side."

"I am glad we'll be in Europe for six months," Gavin chuckled. "That means it will be some time before we see my aunt again. Since both my parents are gone, though she is not my only aunt, she wants to rule my sister's life and mine as she does her only child's."

"I know darling," Veronica said, brushing her cheek on the back of his hand. "Your aunt can indeed be quite difficult to be around."

"Indeed, she's insensitive, always interrupting and barking orders in her high pitched voice, but to think she believed I would marry her daughter is another matter. When I told her I'd never said nor done anything that would indicate more than friendship towards Lillian, my aunt became wholly unreasonable, waving her arms in the air and then pretending to swoon. Her most reprehensible behavior came though, when I further informed her that you and I were to marry. She became so furious that her face turned fiery red, and I thought the old boot was going to die of apoplexy."

"I suppose that reaction is to be expected when one spends one's life trying to marry off a sickly daughter who is without hope of finding a husband on her own." Veronica fanned herself to wave off the heat. "Poor Lillian, I suspect she owes her poor health to her mother's domineering ways."

As they talked, Gavin removed his brown linen jacket and loosened his silk cravat. "I find my aunt's ways insufferable. She might, perhaps, be an agreeable woman but for her incessant prattling and interference. Poor Lillian indeed, I think my cousin might be quite tolerable if her mother would give her a chance to think for herself."

"Then there is my mother," Veronica added as she removed her blue silk shawl and laid it next to her. "As much as I love her, she is far too impressed with peoples' wealth. Fortunately Father does not share her opinions. My mother actually liked Lady Ramsay, despite the fact that she was curt and very demeaning in her opinion of our parlor at Hedgerow; Mother sees only the money. Then of course there's Harriet and Louisa to consider. I'm sorry to say they aren't what one might refer to as accomplished, and they certainly don't have men of fortune waiting in line to ask for their hands. If only my sisters would try harder at becoming more proficient in their studies, but they neither seek, nor are concerned about worthy prospects.

Harriet cares little for a beau. She bores me and my family reciting trite clichés she reads from her tedious books. Additionally, for fear of hurting her feelings, no one has ever had the heart to tell her that she should refrain from singing. As for Louisa, she cannot see past a man in uniform. She has a voice like an angel, but she quivers so badly when performing that she refuses to do more than plunk away at the piano in private. I think both sisters take delight in vexing my mother over these matters."

Gavin chuckled. "When we have our New Year's Eve ball, there may be a few young men who will take an interest in your sisters. But if not, you may set your mother at ease and inform her that I shall have no hesitation in taking care of her and her daughters if the need arises."

"Thank you darling, I'll be sure and tell her of your kindness and generosity. Then perhaps she'll remain silent concerning the subject of matrimony. You have settled my heart immeasurably," Veronica sighed contentedly. "Naturally, I too wish for my sisters' happiness."

"Your sister Colette's marriage to my dear friend Basil Vance could turn out to be an unfortunate alliance where his sister, Miss Phoebe is concerned."

"I couldn't agree with you more," Veronica rustled her lace petticoats hoping to stir some air up around her knees. "Fortunately, Colette is aware of Miss Phoebe's faults and realizes that if allowed she will always be a thorn in her side and mine as well."

"How is it so for you?"

"Well darling, not only did Lady Ramsay desire for you to take her daughter's hand in marriage, I know for a fact that Miss Phoebe seriously hoped you might ask for hers. She tried to make me believe it on more than one occasion when you first began to call on me."

"The nerve of that hussy," Gavin laughed heartily. "Forgive me, I did not mean to say such a thing about my best friend's sister. In truth however, I'm not really surprised to hear that about her; I think I would have expected nothing less."

Veronica grinned, "I knew better than to take her seriously, seeing as Miss Phoebe despises country society in general and the Stuart sisters in particular. She is jealous of our good fortune, and certainly of her brother's marriage to a country girl who has nothing more to recommend her than her beauty and accomplishments."

"Indeed, and it is just the other way around for Miss Phoebe." Gavin pursed his sensual mouth, "Forgive me for saying so, but she has only her fortune to offer to whoever is up for the taking, which so far is no one."

Veronica spoke with disdain, wrinkling her nose in disgust. "Without a doubt, Miss Phoebe has a great deal of pride and false opinion of herself, which prevents her from seeing the truth of her own meanness. I suppose justice would be served in her case if she were, perhaps, to marry a military man. I dare say, she considers herself far too good for anyone in uniform; she as much as said so to Colette. Alas, I fear she will never forgive me for winning your heart."

"In this matter I feel sorrier for Colette than you. You have me to protect you from Miss Phoebe, whereas Basil must in some cases defend his odious sister."

"Thank you my love, I am glad I can count on you," Veronica said longing for a cool breeze. "My, it truly is quite warm. What do you say to enough of our unfortunate friends and relations? Let's not spoil our ride any further by discussing such tedious matters."

"That is a very good idea." Gavin grimaced at the heat in the carriage. "You are quite right about the heat. I can't decide if it's better to have the dust from an open window or the stifling air confronting us as we ride."

"Why don't you open the window a little more? We can always wash the dust off."

"Of course, why not dearest," Gavin said as he leaned over and kissed her tenderly; her deep sigh pleased him.

While traveling through green rolling hills and scenic landscapes during the long days it took to ride from Calais to Paris, Gavin considered his good fortune in winning Veronica's hand. *Who would have believed that I could find such happiness in her arms,* he thought. *How I adore her spontaneity, wit and intellect. Her singing is that of a dove, which surpasses everything but her natural beauty, a beauty I never tire of studying though she discounts it with modesty.*

He had met her through his best friend, Basil Vance, Miss Phoebe's brother. Basil owned a stately country home, Glenvalley, which was a fifteen-minute carriage ride from Hedgerow, the Stuart family's modest five acre estate near Broomfield. When Basil and Gavin met at Oxford, Basil had often spoken of Veronica and her sisters; he was especially fond of Colette.

One day Gavin came home with Basil during a school break and met Veronica. *I remember her like it was yesterday—her radiant, brown eyes with long lashes, and her sensuous mouth when she spoke with eloquence. For months I could not forget the image of her hour-glass figure in that soft pink gown, how it highlighted her porcelain-like neck and ample bosom. How disappointed I was to learn that she had plans to marry her childhood sweetheart.*

Consequently, after meeting Veronica, Gavin felt his chances with her were slim. Most young ladies considered him very handsome, but many were partial solely because of his fortune. He believed this was not the case with Veronica, and he found her lack of interest intriguing; he had never met anyone quite so un-flattered by his attentions.

Another two years passed before he saw her again; she had just turned nineteen and he was twenty-four. When he saw her at Glenvalley, he discovered that she had not married her childhood friend, although her indifference to his own fortune and city manners had not changed. This fascinated Gavin, as did her candor, something he was quite unaccustomed to in young ladies of good breeding.

Finally after six more months and frequent visits to Basil's Glenvalley Estate, Gavin was determined to become better acquainted with Veronica. During a ball that Basil and Miss Phoebe held for the country gentry, Gavin had asked Veronica if he could call on her. The opportunity to see more of her had made him very happy. At the same time he had also been relieved to escape being around Miss Phoebe, who constantly complained and made thoughtless remarks about the Stuart sisters and their lack of urban refinement. With a picture of Miss Phoebe in mind Gavin started to chuckle.

"What amuses you so, darling?" Veronica asked.

"I was just thinking of when I first began to call on you at Hedgerow, and of Miss Phoebe. I laugh because she suddenly reminded me of an upside down broom."

Veronica burst out in gales of laughter. "You're shameless, but it's so true. I never thought of her in that light. It's a perfect description. I must remember to tell Colette."

"Please don't put it in writing," Gavin pleaded. "Should such a portrayal fall into her brother's hands, I would be mortified."

"Of course I would not dare. I thought the very same thing and will only mention it when we see each other. I too would be greatly embarrassed if he were to read such a thing in a letter from me."

Chapter 2

Riding along through French country hamlets, Veronica looked on with interest as they passed peasant families with children playing in ragged clothes. While the men travailed in the hot sun, the women wearing once white aprons took the opportunity to escape their dingy cottages and chatter with each other in the market place.

It amused Veronica, who spoke fluent French and Italian as did Gavin, to hear the locals talk about them as they passed by. "Look Gavin," she said gazing out the window. "The children are pointing at us, saying 'Come see the rich young couple!'"

"I'm pleased that you enjoy the countryside. It doesn't seem much different than England, does it?"

When they reached the industrial town of Amiens, they planned to stop at an inn that had been recommended to them. Amiens, a main thoroughfare to Paris, was known for its poverty from the ravages of war, religious bigotry, disagreeable commoners, and streets full of beggars. The suggested inn sat near one of the town's many sordid, ramshackle neighborhoods. Despite this, the inn was quite charming with its thatched roof, numerous red curtained windows and a columned porch, which spanned the length of the cottage like establishment.

As the honeymooners stepped from the luxurious, red velvet interior of their large, black carriage to check into the inn, two little boys crept underneath the arm of Gavin's footman. The urchins, with hands and faces as dirty as their shabby clothes and bare feet, tried to pick Gavin's pocket.

"I dare say," Gavin demanded stopping them just short of their target. "What do you think you're about?"

The terrified scamps tried to run but were caught by a foul smelling, giant-size man who appeared from out of nowhere. "I got you, you little varmints," he said coarsely, holding them by the scruff of the neck. "How dare you accost this gentleman!"

Veronica covered her mouth with her handkerchief and stared at the children. "Gavin, they can't be more than four or five years old, and they look half starved."

The younger of the two boys sputtered in French street language that they had not eaten all day. Further, he said that 'ma mere', pointing in the direction of a nasty slum, had not done so either. It was a despicable little corner of the world, where a frazzled and tattered woman stood at the entrance of a hut.

Just then the short, pudgy innkeeper came rushing out, fearful that his rich, prospective guests might have been frightened off. "Here, here!" he thundered, "what's the meaning of this?"

The innkeeper changed his tone when he saw the two street urchins dangling side by side from the enormous hand of the huge man. "I'll get you something to eat in a minute. Wait here with Boris and let me settle my guests."

The pleasant innkeeper bowed to Gavin and Veronica. "My name's Higgins and this here's me beautiful inn, The Morningside, fit for a honeymooning pair such as yourselves, it is. Come in, come in. We'll take care of you just as if in beautiful Pariee," Higgins said in his thick cockney accent. "I was born and raised in England but married a pretty French woman. When she died several years ago she left me this Inn. I run it the way I like now, exactly as an English gentleman such as you sir would want."

Veronica whispered to Gavin about the squirming little boys, "They're so pitiful. I know it's the common thing to ignore them, but would you object to my giving the mother a few francs?"

Still holding the scamps, the tall, homely man, Boris, stood quietly oblivious to the kicking and squealing. "Mr. Higgins," Gavin said motioning to the boys, "my man can take the little ones. We'll just be a few minutes. As you see, my wife has a concern for them."

Higgins nodded, "Boris, give the boys to the gentleman's servant. It's all right, you can hand them over."

Gavin told his coachman to take the waifs. "Geeves, you wait here with Rogers. Hold on to them until we come back." His well groomed, uniformed men waited patiently, while the two children twisted and turned, trying desperately to get away.

"I quite agree with you darling. Please, give the woman whatever you wish of this." He smiled lovingly and handed Veronica a purse full of French bank notes. "I must say, it warms my heart to see you troubled. Most young ladies I know would be horrified and think only of themselves were they confronted by beggars."

"Oh Gavin, I'm glad you agree. Do you think it would be all right to personally give the money to the mother? She needn't know our names."

"I see no harm in it, and yes it's good to remain anonymous. Rogers and Geeves can follow us with the boys."

Astonished eyes watched Gavin and Veronica as they went towards the wretched dwelling where the youths said they lived. There a woman with dark circles under her eyes and filthy, yellow hair hanging in them, leaned up against a nauseating blanket that covered the opening to the shack. Her clothes barely hung on her for the rags they were, but her haughty, proud expression implied that she did not belong in such a stench. She would not speak to her soon-to-be benefactors when they asked if the two squealing boys were hers. She only nodded and waved the children into the hut.

"We wanted you to have this," Veronica said, handing her five bank notes, each worth a hundred francs.

It was a large fortune to someone who in the last few years had not scraped together enough money to buy a decent meal for her family. The pitiable woman grabbed the money, went immediately into the shanty and began to sob.

Veronica and Gavin could hear her sons comforting her. "There now mother," they said in perfect English. "Don't cry. We told you everything would be all right someday."

"The woman's name is Shirley Lucile Wagner," Higgins told them, untying his white apron. "She calls herself Lucy; she taught the boys reading and figures—everything. She told me she was educated as a governess, but then she ran off to marry the boys' father without knowing a thing about the scoundrel, poor baggage." Higgins sighed, fiddling with his pipe. "I don't want to say she brought it on herself by doing such a foolish thing, nevertheless, when the husband died she had no family or friends to turn to."

"What brought her here," Gavin asked. "Do you know?"

"She says she escaped to France on a frigate from Dover heading for Calais. It took her a year to make it to our fair town. She was so ragged and worn, she couldn't even make herself presentable enough to get a job, and certainly not with two little tykes." Higgins sucked on his black pipe, the sweet aroma attaching itself to the smell of roast lamb. "The boys speak the street language here. The other scamps won't have nothing to do with them if they talk like proper little Englishmen. Lucy don't say much, except to me, because I turned a sympathetic ear to her. I give them what food I can spare, and I let em stay in that hut, which belonged to my wife. It doesn't cost me anything to help out."

"What did the boy's father do before he died?" Veronica asked.

"He was a merchant from Dover, but when things went sour, he drank himself to death." Higgins frowned, rubbing his bearded face, as he offered his patrons a glass of port and poured himself one. "The husband left her penniless, deep in debt and with babies who were then but two and three years old.

"She told me they escaped the grasps of the law after they'd come to escort her to the courts. She would have been sent to debtors' prison for certain. They found her huddled in a corner of their empty flat holding the boys close to her. There was no more food or money. On the way to court the men turned their backs on her because of a commotion on the other side of the street. She immediately seized the opportunity to flee to a nearby ship and sailed the Channel as a stowaway. Never to be discovered, the ship she hid on left port long before the police thought to look there. Then, as I said, it took her a year to beg her way from Calais to Amiens. She told me she's going to Paris someday."

"A very sad story indeed," Gavin said.

"To know that one of our country women has had such misfortune is truly disheartening." Veronica sighed heavily. "It could just as well have been one of my silly sisters, particularly Gabriella. Had the scoundrel she eloped with been any less worthy, the same might have happened to her. I can only hope that someone would have helped her, as we have this Shirley, I mean Lucy woman."

"Well my darling," Gavin chuckled sipping his wine, "as we decided during our ride through the countryside, we should try not to let unpleasant family affairs intrude on our honeymoon happiness."

"I think I'll be very glad to think as little as possible of them while we're away."

The remainder of their stay at the inn was uneventful. And though not elegant, their accommodations were clean, and the newlyweds were too much in love to notice anything else.

Chapter 3

"We have been here in Paris now for two weeks, and I cannot believe how much we have seen," Veronica declared as she and Gavin sat on the balcony of their hotel suite at the lavish Hotel de Montmorency. "The works of Rembrandt and the Palais du Louver, both are spectacular, but I think the opera was the best. You know more than anything my father would have enjoyed hearing Beethoven perform."

"My father too, preferred Beethoven to Mozart and the Sacre Coeur Cathedral to all others," Gavin said as they sat drinking coffee and watching the people stroll beneath them. "I think my favorite sites are the Pantheon and Notre Dame cathedral."

Veronica gazed at the city skyline. "I have an idea; let's have a picnic on the banks of the River Seine. The hotel can make us a basket lunch."

He laughed as he bit into a flaky piece of mouth-watering pastry. "I think that is a wonderful idea."

Two days later they ventured to the river for their picnic, which the Hotel Montmorency had put together for them. The food basket contained roast beef, baked chicken, crusty breads and jam, fresh apple tarts and a wonderful bottle of vintage red wine.

"I hope your sister is enjoying her stay in Bath while we're away," Veronica said sitting next to Gavin as they watched the Seine flow by. "Does she have many friends there?"

"I believe she has a few, but she spends most her time with our cousin, Captain Bradford. He takes her out often, and I'm sure through him she meets some very nice people. Then again, my aunt has numerous friends also, some of whom have daughters Audrey's age."

"Hasn't she written to you about one young man in particular? I think you said Farnsworth was his name?"

"Yes. He's a friend of the Captain's. By the way, my cousin wrote that Audrey has invited this Farnsworth fellow to join us for Twelfth Night. I hope you don't mind?"

"Not at all," Veronica smiled, thinking how much she liked her new sister-in-law. "There will be lots of family and friends around, and why shouldn't Audrey have a friend as well?"

"You are right, of course," he said, savoring a bite of warm tart. "I didn't see your friend Miss Rosemary at our wedding. Did you hear from her before we left for our honeymoon? I ask, because I'm curious to know how she is holding up under my aunt's wrath over our marriage. Is Miss Rosemary able to abide being Lillian's companion with my aunt always present?"

"She said she's enduring, but she was most sorry to have missed our wedding. She wrote that she and Lillian, who she's very fond of, take many walks together and spend a great deal of time in their park to escape her mother. Rosemary is glad for the occupation, since at age twenty-eight she's considered a spinster; and indeed, she is not inclined to be a governess. Being a companion to Lillian is ideal for her."

Gavin took Veronica's hand to help her stand. "I am pleased that my cousin has a friend. More importantly, I'm glad we have each other." He took her in his arms, and they kissed for a long, passionate moment, until a cool breeze coming off the river interfered with their serenity, as did the servants shuffling about to pack the picnic things.

The next day, just before they were to go to the dressmaker for Veronica's new ball gowns, she received a letter from her sister Colette. "Oh Gavin, Basil has asked his sister, Miss Phoebe, to move out," she said sharing the news with him. "But Colette won't give me the details until we see them at Twelfth Night. I'm eager to know the reason. I think newlyweds should not have to share their first year together with odious in-laws." She covered her mouth in mock shame, "I am sorry darling; I did not mean to speak ill again of your best friend's sister."

"That's quite all right. You might have spoken unkindly, but you did indeed speak the truth." Gavin laughed reaching out for his bride's hand. "No doubt, Miss Phoebe brought it upon herself, whatever the reason."

"Colette said she didn't want to spoil my happiness with unpleasant details."

"Your sister is most thoughtful." He chuckled and pulled Veronica to him. "Now for that trip to the dressmaker, are you ready to go?"

Following six weeks in Paris, the honeymooners traveled to Vienna, Austria where they enjoyed the quaint beauty and peacefulness of the countryside. During their stay, the local gentry extended them an invitation to attend a ball.

"They say that Vienna is where the waltz began," Veronica said standing in front of her mirror admiring her blue, silk ball gown and her diamond necklace, an engagement gift from Gavin.

"You look absolutely perfect tonight," he said looking over her shoulder at her reflection in the mirror. "And yes the waltz was introduced in Vienna in 1776 by the Spanish composer, Vicente Martin I Soler in his Italian Opera "Una Cosa Rara". The dance has been popular in Vienna since then, but it did not arrive in London until 1791. I'm anxious to show you how wonderful it is."

"I've heard it referred to as quite scandalous."

"Many consider it immoral," Galvin laughed straightening his black waistcoat. "They feel this way because of how the partners hold each other so closely for the length of the dance. Some say the movements appear wild and untamed; they claim the waltz has no style. It's very easy to learn. This, of course, does not please dance masters who earn their living by teaching complicated dance steps required for the sarabonde, the minuet or the gaviote."

"Therefore," Veronica stood from her chair and turned toward Gavin, "can one suppose that it is perhaps the English dance masters who spread the idea that the waltz is immoral? Surely here it's not considered indecent, is it?"

"You have a point about the dance masters, but I don't think these Europeans would stand for prudish judgments on a dance that is so well liked."

At the ball Veronica and Gavin glided effortlessly around the ballroom. "You're doing beautifully," he said, marveling at how gracefully and easily she followed his lead. "It's as if you knew how to waltz all along. I believe we should ask for a copy of this music and bring it back to England with us for our first ball together at our Ivywood estate. What do you think about that?"

She laughed softly showing even, white, teeth. "I think that would be delightful. It will stir up quite a commotion, and it will be great fun to see the look of astonishment on the faces of our family and friends. Indeed, what a wonderful surprise for everyone."

"Shocking, to say the least; I'm pleased you approve of the idea. As soon as we arrive home, I'll have the music delivered to the orchestra that plays for our annual New Year's Eve Ball. I will show you off to our guests and be the envy of my friends from London. They will be thrilled by the introduction of the waltz, though the majority of our guests, of course, will not approve."

After dancing several more waltzes, Gavin and Veronica walked over to talk with their hosts, Duke and Duchess Friedrich Von Ruhr from Germany. Veronica liked the Von Ruhr's, and just as she was about to tell them how much she was enjoying the ball, she noticed a heavyset man strutting towards them.

"Oh no," Lady Von Ruhr said in her deep, gentle voice, "it's the impudent Baron Ebert from the Swiss Confederation of Lausanne. I am afraid we cannot stop him from meeting you."

The boastful Baron swaggered up to Gavin and patted him on the back. "My boy," bald Ebert roared, leering at Veronica, his mouth wide and his grin lecherously visible beneath his bushy, red mustache. "You're not going to keep this beautiful young lady all to yourself are you?"

Veronica backed away, swooning from the reek of alcohol on his putrid breath.

"Take your leave now sir," Gavin ordered. "I'm utterly astounded by your unconscionable manners sir. If you do not remove yourself from our presence immediately you will suffer the consequences."

The tall, imposing Von Ruhr stepped forward. "I demand that you apologize to our esteemed guests at once." He rested his hand on his sword, ready to remove it from its scabbard if necessary.

Ignoring the order, the Baron slithered past the general and put his arm around Veronica's waist, forcing her onto the dance floor.

"You horrid man," she said trying to struggle free.

"We'll have none of your refusals now my pretty," Ebert sniggered.

Gavin hotly pursued him with Duke Von Ruhr close behind.

"Take your hands off my wife," Gavin said with deadly calm.

"And if I don't? Lord Hunter is it? What are you prepared to do about it?" The besotted Baron slurred his mighty words and let out a loud belch.

"Swords, right now, outside," Gavin declared.

At this the baron let go of Veronica and drew his weapon. "What's wrong with right here!" he bellowed belligerently. "Draw! Or I'll brand you a coward."

Dueling in England had been outlawed for many years, and Gavin never carried a blade. However, there were men in uniform present with theirs, including Duke Von Ruhr. With his in hand he made ready to defend the integrity of his prestigious guest.

"Sir, this is my wife's honor he has affronted." Gavin bowed to Von Ruhr. "Please allow me to accept the challenge, though I would prefer not to duel in front of the ladies."

The intoxicated baron rallied with sword in hand. "I say, are you, or are you not, a coward sir? The ladies won't mind a little excitement." With that he began to brandish his weapon recklessly and shouted, "The first cut gains the honor!"

Von Ruhr obliged and handed Gavin his sword. Veronica watched in horror as her husband began circling the baron. The graceful, slender Lady Hildred Von Ruhr, almost as tall as her husband, put her arm around Veronica.

"Don't worry my dear; the baron is no match for Lord Hunter. I must say his reputation as a gentleman of charm and valor fits him perfectly. To be sure, your husband knows what he's doing; see his precision and expert handling of the sword."

Veronica stared at her quizzically and wondered. *How can she be so glib? I cannot fathom it. Nevertheless, her elegant informality and genuine smile does offer some degree of calmness.*

"Yes, yes, I understand your concern," Lady Von Ruhr continued with her hand on Veronica's shoulder. "As soon as this is over the Baron will be removed from the premises and will not be invited to another affair in all of Vienna unless it is to a tavern brawl. You have my word on it."

Standing at the perimeter of the ballroom the guests stared as the swordsmen went to it, swaggering and jabbing, handing a couple of near misses on the way. It seemed to Veronica as if the fighting went on forever, but in reality it was only about five minutes. Indeed, the Baron's intoxicated state coupled with his rotund shape clearly affected his ability to wield the sword, and Gavin easily out maneuvered him at every turn.

Baron Ebert huffed and puffed as he laboriously tried to parry at Gavin's thrust, but then the Baron dropped his sword. When he managed to bend over and make contact with it, Gavin, two steps ahead of him, used his own sword to catch the tip of Ebert's and tossed it high into the air. The blade flew almost to the height of the twenty-five foot ballroom ceiling. When the sword plunged toward the floor, Gavin caught it with his free hand and shrewdly, but with care, gave Ebert a keen slash on the cheek. Mortified by the cut with his own foil, the baron made a perfunctory bow before being escorted out of the room by two brutish looking servants.

A sigh of admiration for the victor came from the on-lookers as Gavin handed the weapon back to Von Ruhr. "I thank you sir for its use," Gavin said taking his bow. Then he turned to Veronica. "You needn't have worried darling, but I see that you are. Shall we retire for the evening?"

"I am sorry; I did not mean to look distressed. Truly, I'm fine, and relieved that the contemptible Baron is gone. If you'd like I would not mind another waltz," she declared, fanning her flushed face.

"Bravo!" Duke Von Ruhr patted Gavin on the back. "Now, please accept our apology for such rude behavior on the part of our impossible guest. We are delighted you have chosen to stay."

Gavin and Veronica spent another six weeks in Vienna. They saw the sights of Hofburg, the Imperial palace of the Royal Habsburg family and took evening rides in an open carriage to watch the sun set over the serene Danube River. And they were invited to many balls by the Von Ruhrs, in whose villa they stayed as guests.

Chapter 4

"I am truly sorry to say goodbye to our new friends in Austria," Veronica said as they rode out of town heading for Venice. I hope Italy will be as wonderful."

"You will love Venezia, as they say." Gavin sighed, drinking in the cool morning breeze coming through the carriage windows. "The canals there are amazing, and the shores of the Adriatic Sea belong to this beautiful city. You'll find it all quite enchanting." He laughed and touched her cheek, "Of course nothing in nature is as beautiful as you."

Veronica sighed smiling up at Gavin. "You are too generous with your praise darling, but thank you. Now I can hardly wait to see this city you rave about. I've heard that the men who drive the boats down the waterways are very serious."

"The boats are gondolas and the men who steer them are called gondoliers. Indeed, they are quite serious about their famed profession, and though poor, their ancient skill makes them very proud."

Their first evening on the Grand Canal Veronica watched with fascination, as the boatmen rounded turns chanting carnal pleas and arcane tunes, while their bodies swayed to the rhythm of the oars.

"Can't you just feel romance in the air," Veronica said, giddy with happiness as she lounged under the canopy of their skiff.

"I can indeed," Gavin whispered helping her with her silk cape.

She giggled and squirmed as he wrapped his arms around her and began nibbling on her ear. "Really Gavin, we don't want to spill into the canal, do we? And should you do such things to me in public?"

"We won't turn out, and this isn't public, darling. We're hidden from view of the gondolier, remember?" he said pointing upward. "As to romance, it is quite normal for Venice. Every guest that comes here can feel its decadent, but loving, air all around. Now," he laughed, "inasmuch as we have this privacy on such an idyllic night, I think I want to trade places with you so that I can nibble your other ear."

They both laughed as they twisted and turned changing seats, but the mood was momentarily spoiled when the irritated gondolier barked at them. "Are you trying to turn us over? If you don't cease this rocking we will surely end up in the water."

With these words of admonishment, the tall thin guide on his gilded bark lost his footing and nearly fell into the canal, as his passengers shifted their bodies again. "Did you not hear me?" the oarsman said harshly, his squinty eyes peering at them under the canopy. "I must insist that you sit still or you'll be delivered to the nearest dock."

"My apologies sir," Gavin said. "Please accept this as a token of my sincerity." He handed him a lira for the inconvenience.

For the remainder of their ride the young lovers endeavored to contain their laughter over the near mishap. But soon, as they looked out at the stars they laughed out loud in agreement.

"It's difficult to distinguish our man from the tall oar he uses to guide the boat," Gavin whispered, stifling his laugh with his hand. "I'm sure if he heard us snickering at him now, he would most certainly drop us off post haste, despite my tip."

Veronica began to laugh with little composure, and when Gavin asked her why, she squeaked out in a whisper, "I suddenly had a vision of Miss Phoebe marrying someone like our swaggering gondolier." She caught her breath and added, "I know it's unkind of me to even think such a thing, but I couldn't help myself."

"It's an amusing thought indeed," Gavin agreed. "I'm reminded of kindling for firewood."

Veronica erupted into hearty laughter. In hopes of not being forced out onto an unknown pier, Gavin tried without success to keep her still.

"I must insist that you take your leave at the next pier," the gondolier announced. "It is the entrance to the city's finest hotel. I clearly warned you that I would not tolerate your moving around in this craft, as I have no intention of finding myself in the canal."

He proceeded to dock the boat, stepped out and helped Veronica and Gavin to the platform. Then he surprised them by handing Gavin back his tip. "I cannot accept this. Your safety and mine is more important than a gratuity." He bowed haughtily and silently stepped back into his gondola.

Though a little surprised that the man had been true to his word, the honeymooners did not tell him that the palatial hotel, where he dropped them was where they were staying.

After utopian Venice, the Hunters made their way to the extraordinary metropolis of Rome. "I believed there was nothing like London or Paris," Veronica said. "I've heard that Rome has over three hundred churches and more palaces and amphitheaters than I could ever count."

"And they're not only within the city walls, but outside as well," Gavin said, enjoying her enthusiasm. "I felt the same as you when I came here as a student. I too was taken in by this city's vast mixture of peasants, priests, and noblemen. Wait until you see the world famous coliseum."

"I'm eager to see it all," she said, turning to look at the bigger than life statue of two Greek gods trying to master sea horses; in the background sat the Arch de Triumph. "What is the fountain's name?"

"The Fontanna di Trevi, and those are Tritons attempting to control the horses. The Tritons represent two moods of the sea, one is placid, and the other is clearly restless. Visitors from everywhere throw coins over their shoulder into the water. They say it will ensure a future stay in the city."

"Shall we toss a coin in too?"

"All right darling, if you like."

They each threw a handful of lira into the fountain, and five little urchins immediately jumped in after them. "This English couple must be very rich," one boy said. "Or perhaps they have a very big wish." The other children laughed and splashed water all over each other trying to grab as many coins as they could.

Gavin chuckled when he saw the look of surprise on Veronica face. "The children are fearless aren't they?"

"There's hardly time for the coins to settle," she observed, clearly amused by the activity in the fountain. "I read that Rome was once a city of affluence, but that it also has a profusion of artists, tradesmen, criminals, beggars, and prostitutes, as well as numerous priests."

"'Tis true my dear. And there are many tourists just like you and I, either on their honeymoon or seeking antiquities. Now since you mention artists, I wanted to surprise you and have your portrait painted during our stay. There are some very famous painters here; I'll inquire about one when we visit either the Gallery of St. Luca or the Doria Pamphili Gallery. Both should house a few good artists. We'll ask."

"I've always thought it would be nice to have my likeness on canvas. Colette told me in her last letter that Basil arranged to have hers painted as well."

The next day they visited the Gallery of St Luca and spoke with the steward, a tall, pompous man with a pointy, black beard. "I am sure Lord Hunter that for the right price, Jean Duveaux would oblige your request. He is of local renown and is here as we speak. I'd be happy to make the introduction."

When they met the bushy headed Duveaux, with more hair than muscle, he happily agreed to paint Veronica's portrait at his studio.

"But," he laughed crudely sucking in a deep breath, "only because she is very beautiful will I do this. And of course, I will charge you a large sum of money. Your wife is worth the price, yes?"

They arranged for her to sit in Duveaux's musty studio for three hours every day until he was done. He said it would be two weeks, but in fact it took nearly four. "She is much too beautiful for me to hurry," the feisty painter said everyday to Gavin. "A good painter cannot rush this sort of thing."

When it was finished, Gavin admitted that it was worth the wait as he admired the way Duveaux had secured Veronica's lovely face and pleasing countenance. He paid the man five hundred lira, with an additional hundred to show his gratitude.

Nearing the end of their trip the Hunters continued their honeymoon in Madrid. "I had no idea how large this city was, and I did not envision its grandeur," Veronica sighed viewing some of the sights of the huge metropolis. "I truly adore these spacious parks and shady promenades." She fanned herself as she looked out the carriage window trying hard to take everything in at once. "I can't wait to walk down the Museo del Prado Boulevard. Madrid is like Rome in many ways, with streets cooled by numerous fountains and lined by lush trees."

"It is a splendid city, but its grandness is equaled in magnitude only by the poverty found in its many narrow, squalid streets. The city hosts a citizen population of over two hundred thousand in addition to half again as many foreigners. And I'm told," Gavin pointed to the frequent carriages that passed by, "that one might often see up to four hundred coaches drive by each day."

"I think the most romantic thing here is the Madrilènes that serenaded us last evening after supper."

"Like Venice, Madrid is truly a city filled with passion," Gavin agreed. "Would you like to get out and walk now? This street is known as Meadow Walk by the English tourists. By the way," Gavin said feeling the heat of the day as he adjusted his cravat. "I meant to tell you, the steward at the hotel told me of a quaint inn that offers fine cuisine and exciting entertainment. Do you think you might enjoy dining there? It's called the Villanueva de Madrilènes and is famous for its vibrant music and fascinating Spanish dancers."

"It sounds delightful."

The following evening they dined at the Villanueva, a crowded inn filled with noblemen and commoners alike all chattering at once. As soon as Gavin and Veronica were brought their lamb stew with crusty bread and a hearty burgundy wine, two Spaniards pulled a supper table to the forefront of the inn, jumped onto it and began a dance competition. Both men, tall and lanky, one with sideburns to his neck and the other nearly bald, tapped to the music of guitars. They moved their feet so fast that Veronica could not take her eyes away, she was mesmerized by the rhythm and speed of the swiftest moving feet she'd ever seen.

After the competition ended and the applause stopped, a disturbance emerged from a corner of the room. Two angry men, one a tall brawny man with a mug of ale in his hand, the other, skinny and well dressed smoking a pipe, argued loudly over which of the dancers they thought was best. Soon their conversation turned into shouting and not long after they drew their swords.

When one of the men slashed the arm of the other, blood immediately stained the white billowy sleeve of his shirt. Gavin saw the fear in Veronica's eyes, despite the poorly lit room.

"I see you're not amused," he said. "We shall leave at once."

As soon as they started for the door the fighters began moving in that direction as well. The stout proprietor of the establishment tried, but to no avail, to have the men take their dispute outside. Ignoring him, they proceeded to knock over tables, spill the wine and break the goblets, as plates were smashed and food went flying.

Concerned for his wife's safety, Gavin took her by the hand and headed for the kitchen. "We'll go through the back," he whispered.

As they stepped outside, Veronica was overcome with fear. "It is pitch dark out here," she said just as a woman screamed and a dog growled near by.

"We best go back," Gavin said and swiftly pulled Veronica inside.

They returned to the dining area and dead silence. The fighting had stopped, but the tall brawny man lay on the floor gasping for air as blood ran from his mouth.

One of the guests, a dark bearded Englishman, leaned over to Gavin and remarked, "He was surprised by the pistol the gentleman pulled from his shirt. Shot him in cold blood, he did. 'Tis murder indeed!"

In his dying breath the injured fighter called out his last words, "You blackguard, you'll rot in hell for this."

Veronica fainted and Gavin carried her out the front door to their waiting carriage, angry with himself for having brought her to such a place. The innkeeper followed them out bowing and making his sincerest apologies.

The next day the Hunters left Madrid ahead of schedule. "I want to be as far away from this place as possible Gavin, and I don't think we can leave soon enough."

"You're quite right my dear. I regret that you had to witness such violence last night," Gavin said caressing her hand as they rode out of town.

They traveled to Lisbon on the Atlantic Coast where they spent five days. Gavin made arrangements with the captain of her Majesty's Royal Navy whose ship was docked in the Port of Lisbon. He and Veronica were granted passage to sail back to England with them.

"It's like we're already home Gavin." Veronica let out a deep sigh, feeling relieved and happy standing on the deck of the handsome craft enjoying the breeze on her face. "I am as anxious as ever to have my feet on English soil again, but I want you to know darling that I've enjoyed every moment of our trip. I shall never forget how wonderful you have been to me. Everything was perfect, thank you."

"You are entirely welcome, my love," Gavin replied with unsinkable joy in his heart. "I have to insist though, that without you by my side the sights would have been dull indeed. Traveling with you during the past six months has been the most wonderful time of my life."

Chapter 5

After being home for several weeks at the Hunter's Ivywood estate, the newlyweds anxiously awaited the arrival of family and friends for Christmas and their Twelfth Night Celebrations. The first week in December Veronica's easy-going sister, Colette, and her good natured husband, Basil, were the first holiday guests to arrive.

"It is wonderful to see you," Veronica said, hugging Colette with great enthusiasm. "How I've missed you. Seven months is the longest we've ever been apart."

"You both look quite well, despite your four-hour ride." Gavin smiled warmly. "We'll have tea ready for you, and then supper as soon as you've settled in."

After they dined Gavin and Basil went happily to the men's parlor for their brandy, while Veronica and Colette visited in their guest suite. "I adore the yellow and blue colors in here Veronica," Colette said, her jovial, crescent eyes sparkled as she patted the skirt of her gown. "Did you have this done for us, or was it already like this?"

"I've had little time to do much since we arrived home barely four weeks ago. I thought you might like these rooms and decided not to change them right away. However, I have some redecorating plans for the spring," Veronica replied, studying Colette's pleasing countenance. "You can't tell yet that you are five months with child, you look wonderful. How are you feeling?

"Thank you dear sister, I feel quite good. You look very well too."

"I am more content than I ever dreamed possible," she sighed happily.

"And like me, there is no doubt, you are very much in love," Colette giggled blithely. "We succeeded Veronica. Do you realize it dear? We married for love."

"I could not imagine any other way." Veronica felt a tingling of joy thinking of Gavin as she spoke. "Let's pray that our sisters, Louisa and Harriet, do as well, though I have little hope for them. I fear equally for Gabriella, but it is too late for her. Judging by the only two letters I have received since her marriage, I don't think that charlatan she eloped with to Plymouth makes her very happy." Veronica frowned, letting her hair down and running her fingers through it. "Her third letter came just the other day saying they will not be here for the holidays."

"I have to agree with you, for I have not heard from her any more than you. But now I have some good news I have been saving for you." Colette wrapped her blue muslin robe tighter around her as she lounged on a yellow, brocade chaise. "I want you to know that you'll find Louisa and Harriet much improved. I think because of Gabriella's elopement, and since we married well, Father insisted that Louisa and Harriet take further instruction on improving their piano, singing and comportment."

"I am thrilled to have such news," Veronica sighed, feeling relieved. "I have been a little concerned about the impression they might make on some of Gavin's friends. Any enhancement to Harriet's past performances can only be a step up in society for her. As for Louisa, I have never heard her sing at any of our parties. Nevertheless, heaven knows we have too often been humiliated by our sisters' lack of accomplishment and guidance."

"Indeed, and now they are much improved. But you know," Colette added, "I still can't get over Gabriella running off with that man, even if it has been over a year now. 'Tis a shame no one knew him very well."

"Least of all our sister," Veronica frowned.

"I believe Gabriella has made a foolish alliance and is unhappy as you said. Otherwise, would she not write more and describe her bliss? Louisa believes this to be the case too."

"I'm of the same opinion. She's either enjoying married life and is too busy to write, or she's despairing over lack of felicity and has no desire to correspond."

Colette yawned and stood up to get into her bed. "I hope Gabriella is well."

"I pray for the same, daily." Veronica went to sit at the foot of the bed and covered her feet with a small, blue velvet blanket. "Now dearest, you must know how anxious I am to hear all about what happened to Basil and his sister."

"To be sure," Colette laughed. "I have kept you in suspense about Miss Phoebe long enough."

"It was quite unfair of you to have even mentioned it in your letter. So now tell me, did Basil really ask her to move out? Was she horribly odious to you? I know she'd hoped to remain at Glenvalley after your honeymoon, but I'm sure you're as glad as I am that she did not. Clearly, we both know she is jealous of her brother's affections towards anyone but herself."

"And he has little enough for her as it is," Colette replied and started to giggle. "I should not say such a thing, though it is true."

Veronica smiled. "Oh, it's true all right. It has always been obvious to me that Miss Phoebe is deficient in inner beauty, which does not help when one tries to overlook her lack of physical attractiveness."

"As you know, I do try to think the best of people, but I agree with you in her case. When Basil asked her to leave, I was very disappointed in her. She behaved exceptionally ill towards me; in truth her manner was horrid, and I could not really discuss her faults with Basil. After all, she is still his sister. He knows well enough what she is without me pointing out her unpleasantness and disagreeable nature."

"You're absolutely right Colette. It's wise of you not to tell him what you really think."

"When we returned from our wedding trip Miss Phoebe's cordiality towards me was most insincere, but I believed Basil thought she felt some fondness for me. However, about two weeks after you and Gavin left for your honeymoon, she and that Mrs. Mudduglee, the cranky, old housekeeper, conspired against me. They claimed one evening that our dinner goose was ill flavored because it had been prepared according to my instructions. Unmistakably, it tasted dreadful and was over cooked; but I could not believe my ears when Miss Phoebe sat at dinner with us and attempted to put the blame for the miserable goose on me. Well Veronica, you know I would never interfere in the kitchen, it is not my place. Of course, Miss Phoebe wanted only to insult me and make me out to be a common servant."

"She is a wretched woman," Veronica interjected, feeling disgust at such spitefulness. "I can't possibly understand how she can have a brother as amiable as Basil."

"I find it difficult to believe as well, but there is more. My astonishment grew when I heard what Basil said to her after she accused me of the spoiled goose. He told her not to think for one moment that her skullduggery had gone unnoticed by him. He informed her that she and the housekeeper would be leaving at dawn. He suggested Miss Phoebe move in with their sister Ursula and her husband, Mr. Twackham. Poor Miss Phoebe, can you believe that such a thing could happen to her."

"Poor Miss Phoebe indeed," Veronica replied. "I am glad to hear that my brother-in-law has such mettle. Nevertheless, even though she deserved this from your husband, one is obliged to feel a little sorry for her. It is gratifying however, to know that someone finally had the gumption to put her in her place. Who better to do it than her own brother? I dare say she must have been upset."

"Yes, of course, she was mortified, and for once in her life she had nothing to say for herself. She simply got up from the table and left the room. It goes without saying; I was pleased to be rid of both her and that dreadful housekeeper, who we replaced with a very courteous and capable woman that Mother recommended."

"And how are you and Miss Phoebe now. Is she humbled and nicer to you, or is she still a bore?"

"We converse now as if nothing ever happened, though the strain between us has not really lessened." Colette yawned and rubbed her pretty blue eyes. "Now I must get some sleep, dearest. Do you mind if we say good night?"

"Of course not, I am tired as well. I'll wait till morning to share some interesting news from our friend and former neighbor, Rosemary."

"Really," Colette said concerned. "I have not seen Rosemary for several months. I hope she is not unwell."

"She is fine, it's something else. I assure you it is most amusing to Gavin and me."

Colette sighed. "I suppose it can wait until tomorrow. Afterwards, I am anxious to see the new Paris wardrobe you wrote me about, and then I will have my tour of Ivywood as you promised."

"It is wonderful having you here. I cannot wait to show you everything. I've missed you Colette."

"And I, you," she said as they hugged good night.

When Veronica went to her boudoir to prepare for bed, her maidservant, Margaret, had laid her bed clothes out and was waiting patiently to brush Veronica's hair and help her change into her silk nightgown. All through Europe, Margaret, who was twenty eight, had displayed a cheery and sensible disposition. Veronica liked her very much and could not imagine how she had ever done without a servant she did not have to share with her sisters.

This particular night Veronica knew Gavin would continue his visit with Basil for some time. Thus, she snuggled under their down quilts and watched the glow of the fire reflect off the ceiling tiles, as each one displayed a carved rose, painted in red and white, with green leaves. She greatly appreciated such appointments, for growing up she'd had a comfortable living, but nothing at all like the opulence that surrounded her now. *In spite of all the money,* she mused, suddenly feeling very tired, *I quite admire my new life, though I would not want a jot of it without Gavin.*

When Gavin finally came into their bedroom, he went to the bed with candle in hand. Gazing down at his sleeping bride, he knelt beside her to observe her more closely and gently kissed her forehead.

"You're so beautiful," he whispered. "I love you very much."

She rolled onto her side facing him, as her long, soft curls tumbled onto her cheeks without disturbing her sleep. He admired her full lips and sweet smile, but he did not have the heart to wake her. It was the first time they had not gone to bed together since their wedding night.

That evening over brandy, he and Basil had taken great pleasure reminiscing about their honeymoon travels. After that, Gavin had been eager to come to bed with his bride, but now he was unable to fall asleep. He lay there for some time reminiscing about their first weeks together after returning from their honeymoon.

Their first week at home, Gavin had planned a picnic and a tour of Ivywood's extensive grounds. The property consisted of two small lakes, three ponds, a waterfall, several groves of oak and elm trees, wild flowers, tended flowers, and exquisitely trimmed lawns. The morning of the picnic they went to the stables, where they were greeted by the groomsmen holding two horses for them.

"For you darling," Gavin handed her the reins to the stunning, chestnut mare with white socks. "What will you name her?"

She stood speechless and was dazzled for several moments as she rubbed her hand over the neck of the bay. "Gavin you have given me so much already, your generosity overwhelms me. Thank you." She reached up and kissed him on the cheek. "I must call her Sacre Coeur after the cathedral in Paris. Sacre Coeur will remind me of the wonderful time we had in that great city."

"It is a good name." He smiled as he helped her up. "Do you remember me telling you about my favorite stallion, Danube?" he said taking the bridle of a striking black horse. "Here he is."

"He's magnificent."

"I agree." Gavin mounted Danube and motioned for Veronica to follow him to the top of a knoll.

"I wanted you to see the panorama of Ivywood from here," he said when they settled on the bluff. "You can see all seven square miles that it encompasses."

Veronica looked out over the tree tops with the mansion sitting to the left. "It is truly a spectacular view!"

Gavin shaded his eyes and pointed, "You see that grassy dell down there?"

She nodded and spurred Sacre Coeur. "I'll race you."

Not waiting for a reply, she smiled as she flew down the hill ahead of him. *I love the feel of a good mount under me, as well as the breeze blowing on my face.*

"You're amazing," Gavin laughed when she beat him to the dell. "I underestimated your skill with the horse."

"Did you forget that Colette and I used to ride through Charnwood Forest nearly every day before you and I were married?" She giggled and reached out her arms for him to help her down. "I must say that Sacre Coeur is the largest horse I've ever ridden."

"You do sit quite high on her, but she suits you," he said, taking her in his arms and kissing her gently on the forehead. "I have looked forward to this day when we could ride through the grounds of Ivywood together."

"It's extraordinary being here, such magnificence! From the moment I laid eyes on Ivywood, I too have longed to ride through it with you."

Gavin stooped to pick a yellow wild flower. "For your hair," he said with a look of passion in his expressive, blue eyes. "Why don't we sit on the grass for awhile?"

She sighed as he reached for her and kissed her single-mindedly. After reveling in the peace and beauty of their surroundings and each other, they got back on their horses and sauntered off through the rolling landscape filled with faded fall colors; and the gently blowing breeze refreshed them.

Toward lunchtime, with the sun high in the sky and the temperature just right, Gavin turned to Veronica. "I am taking you through a woodsy area, where we'll come upon a spectacular view of a small, secluded lake. It is on the far edge of the estate and there's a surprise for you there."

When they reached the area Gavin spoke of, Veronica exclaimed excitedly, ogling the beauty around her. "It is like paradise here, and the waterfall is perfect. Is that the surprise?"

"Yes! This cove is my private hideaway, and no one but family ever comes here. Some have seen the other side of the fall, but not this hidden cove. My parents used to bring Audrey and me here when we were young."

"I am overwhelmed by the beauty that abounds on the whole of Ivywood, but this is by far the most remarkable place. I love the sound of the cascading water."

"I'm glad we decided not to involve the servants in our picnic. Ordinarily they would have had the food laid out for us, but I think we can manage without them, don't you?"

"Oh yes," Veronica sighed. "This spot is far too intimate to have servants swarming over us."

Their picnic basket seemed a banquet fit for royalty. The wine was superb and the fare delicious, but invariably it was more than either of them could eat. After the meal, Veronica stood up to stretch and undid her coiffure. "It feels good to run my fingers through my hair, though I'm a little sorry to ruin the curls Margaret worked so hard on this morning."

"I like your natural curls loose, especially when we're alone." Gavin smiled, his senses enticed. "You are seductive indeed."

He stood next to her and smoothed her dark tresses with his hands. Then he wrapped his arms around her, and after a few minutes he drew her down beside him. At length the whispering breeze in the trees and the gentle din of the cascading falls stirred them.

Veronica sat up and looked out at the water. "I think I'd like to get my feet wet, but I cannot see a good place to go in."

Gavin motioned to her, "Over here." He leaped onto a large rock. "Here darling, take my hand and stand by me."

Reaching up to him, she missed the step and while trying to catch her, they both plunged into the water. Laughing uproariously, they chased each other through the waterfall and played in the water until Veronica began to shiver.

When they reached dry ground, Gavin frowned with worry. "We better dry you off darling, before you catch your death. Look at you, you're trembling. The temperature has dropped, you best put my jacket on and wrap the picnic cloth around you. Perhaps that will help a little."

"Thank you," she said between chattering teeth.

"Let me give you a foot up onto Sacre Coeur. Then I suggest we race as fast as we can back to dry clothes and a warm fire. The servants can come back for the picnic things."

Once settled in their room with a fire burning brightly, Veronica insisted she would be all right. "I'm fine darling. It has been a wonderful day, thank you."

"I'm glad you enjoyed yourself, I did also. However, I am going to have supper brought up, as I think you should get in bed and keep warm."

"If you wish," Veronica sighed, still feeling chilled. "I'll have Margaret help me change while you see to our meal."

"I'll fetch a servant to tell the kitchen what we want."

He looked back to ensure that she truly was all right. By the time he returned to their room, she was fast asleep.

Chapter 6

Veronica awakened early the morning after Colette and Basil arrived; she looked forward to spending time with her sister before more family and guests came. Sitting in her bath with a robust fire to keep her boudoir warm, Veronica contemplated the matter of Miss Phoebe Vance.

I don't like going to bed with ugly thoughts, but since the morning is fresh, I think it's time to make a decision about Basil's sister. I've experienced her attitude and odious behavior all too often. What a pity that in her arrogance she considers herself worthy of all rich men's attentions, despite her unpleasant personality.

"What a silly woman," Veronica said out loud, luxuriating in her bath.

Just then Margaret, smiling affably, came in with a white towel draped over her arm. "Are you ready for me to wash your back, my lady?"

"Yes, thank you. I was sitting here thinking about a particular guest that will be arriving, and she's of a most disagreeable nature."

"I'm sorry to know that you will have to endure someone so unpleasant in your own home, my lady."

Veronica laughed, relishing Margaret's firm hands as she washed her back. "I am sure I'll manage. She has nothing but disdain for me and my sisters simply because before we married, we lacked fortune and connections; this is despite the fact that we are the daughters of a gentleman."

"How can you abide someone so tiresome?" Margaret asked, her determined round chin jutting out. "Whatever shall be done with a person like that?"

"Well, I've decided to instruct Mrs. Anderson to use name cards for seating around the table at all our meals. Never is the person in question to be placed anywhere near me, Lord Hunter, or my sisters." Veronica laughed. "That should help my disposition while eating at the very least."

"I think that is very wise." Margaret smiled, helping Veronica step out of the tub. "I thought I just heard someone knocking at the door."

"It is Mr. Hunter," Veronica said, pulling on her white silk robe. "I can manage now, Margaret. I'll call for you when I'm ready to have you do my hair."

"Good morning darling," Veronica smiled, tying her robe tightly around her tiny waist.

"I hope I'm not disturbing you?" He kissed her lovingly on the cheek. "I must say you look absolutely beautiful this morning. Thank you for allowing me to come in."

"Thank you, and of course you're not disturbing me. I am delighted to see you, as we did not have a chance to visit last evening. I wanted you to know that I've decided what to do about Miss Phoebe and her sister Mrs. Twackham."

"Really, do you care to share with me?"

"Of course, but first I'll tell you what Colette told me about Miss Phoebe and her brother." Veronica proceeded to relate all that Colette had said. "How Miss Phoebe ever expected to find a husband in the countryside anyway is a mystery to Colette and me."

Gavin laughed. "Given the fact that she despises country society in general, you are quite right."

"Perhaps Basil did her a favor by asking her to leave." Veronica remarked. "He certainly did his wife one."

"Indeed, and I'm glad to see that he saw right through his sister. I think she only wanted to stay with him in order to be a thorn in Colette's side."

Veronica sighed. "I'm certain you're right about that. But, truly, I wonder if this was humiliation enough to cause her to change?"

"I doubt it," Gavin chuckled. "I'll wager she's still as haughty as ever. Now you said you had a plan for Miss Phoebe?"

"To be sure that we don't overestimate any changes on her part, I'll not take my chances." Veronica giggled, and told him about the seating arrangements. "Now darling, I wanted to know if you had a pleasant evening with Basil."

"I did, very much so, though he mentioned nothing of his encounter with his sister. Are you ready to give Colette a tour of Ivywood?"

"First I plan for her to read Rosemary's letter, then I can't wait to show her the manor as well as my new Paris wardrobe. I hope she is well rested because she and I will be busy all day."

After breakfast Veronica gave Colette the letter from their former neighbor, "This will astonish you, dear sister."

"I know Rosemary writes to you, but I don't hear from her," Colette said. "I trust she enjoys her new position as a companion to Gavin's cousin, Lillian Ramsay."

"See for yourself." Veronica handed her the letter.

December 1815
Dear Veronica,
You will never believe what has happened. The other day after visiting my family, I came back to find Lady Ramsay in a rage over shocking news. She was in such a state that she took to her bed, unable to contain her fury. Lillian diligently tried to pacify her, but little good it did.
She asked if I would write to you and inform Mr. Hunter of his new

cousin, her half brother. *The person of whom I speak is a gentleman by the name of Edward Ramsay, recently arrived from America. He is young and handsome Lillian told me, and he claims to be the son of Lady Ramsay's late husband. He presented a signed document proving it, and he had a couple of letters his father had written to him and his mother shortly before he died.*

Apparently as a young man Lord Ramsay, Lillian's father, had married a girl from Bristol. Because she was deemed of little consequence, without fortune or family name, his parents were mortified by the idea of their son marrying such low estate and had the marriage annulled.

However, this being done, they were unaware that the girl was carrying their son's child. Mr. Ramsay told Lillian that according to the letters, his father and mother were very much in love, but his father could do nothing about the nullification of the marriage. Nevertheless, he did set them up with some friends of his in Liverpool. The mother gave birth to her child there, and then she and the baby sailed to America.

What no one but the mother knew, was that the father had given her a secret fortune in diamonds. Lord Ramsay had discovered the diamonds while on a trip to India, but he had told no one about them. With this in hand, the mother and child traveled to meet another friend of Lord Ramsay's in America. The man owned a cotton plantation in South Carolina. Mother and child, along with the diamonds, carried a letter written by Lord Ramsay, acknowledging himself as the father of the baby. In the letter he asked his friend to give them refuge until he could come for them. However he never did, though Mr. Ramsay did not say why.

Over the last ten years Edward Ramsay, who is now twenty-eight, with the help of the diamonds, has amassed a fortune of five hundred thousand pounds. This information came from Lillian to me, and her mother does not know. Lillian said she and her new-found half brother had quite an opportunity to talk while her mother's vapors went on for several days.

Lord Ramsay's acquaintance died about five years ago, leaving his entire estate to Edward Ramsay, whose mother had died four years earlier. These events are partly what caused Mr. Ramsay to return to England.

Of course Lady Ramsay was outraged that her late husband, who I believe died thirteen years ago, never told her that he had been married before. However, the true effrontery came in learning of the son.

Lillian told me in confidence that she liked her half brother exceedingly well and said he seemed quite elated to find his long lost 'family'. Nonetheless, Lady Ramsay's disapproval and poor reception clearly disappointed him. Lillian assures me he's as polished as any English gentleman. I am only sorry I did not have the opportunity to meet him.

Lady Ramsay was so distraught about her stepson's appearance that she and Lillian left to winter in the South of France. I decided to remain behind because, as you know, my uncle in Bath has invited me to spend the holidays with him.

One last thing, Lillian did say that Mr. Ramsay would be paying a visit to his cousin, your Mr. Hunter, very soon. Well there you have it. I shall write you after the holidays and send my love and felicitations for the merriest of Twelfth Night celebrations.

Your Friend, Rosemary

"I'm astonished to read this news," Colette said, handing the letter back. "Can you imagine the shock?"

"Gavin and I are very anxious to meet his cousin. Though I would not say this to Gavin, I think this new step son is a rather fitting form of justice for all the disapproval Lady Ramsay has shown our family. I think everyone needs a little scandal now and then to keep them from feeling superior as Lady Ramsay does."

"I think you may be right, and I'm certain her rebuff to the stepson must have hurt him deeply." Colette shook her head sadly then looked at Veronica with a smile, "But now, let's see that new Paris wardrobe of yours."

They spent the next couple of hours exclaiming over their new clothes and afterwards, they toured the manor. "Did you say," Colette asked, "that you have a hundred and twenty servants on the whole of Ivywood? At Glenvalley there are only seventy-five, and I thought that was a great number."

"It is quite a few, so you can imagine how awed I am by the hundred and twenty we have. However that includes everyone from the carriage house servants and stable attendants to the grounds keepers and household staff. Between Mr. Walton, the steward and Mrs. Anderson, our housekeeper, the manor runs very smoothly because they manage the entire cadre with a firm, but fair, hand."

"First I'll take you to the dining rooms. Of the two the largest one can seat a hundred guests. However, we only dine there when we have a crowd. Most of the time we are served in the smaller one; it is much cozier since it only seats twenty." Veronica grinned as she noticed the look on Colette's face. "What is the matter dearest; you look puzzled?"

"I am just taken in by all this grandeur and find it hard to believe that you are actually the mistress of this place."

"It is amazing isn't it? Now I have a surprise to show you in the gallery." Half way down the long hall Veronica stopped and looked up in awe at a painting, which she had not yet gotten used to seeing.

"Oh Veronica, you look absolutely stunning," Colette ogled as she stared at the life size portrait of her sister, which hung next to Gavin's.

"We are pleased with it." Veronica told Colette where they had it painted and about the feisty artist who took four weeks to do it. Gavin says it completes this hall perfectly until the next Hunter generation arrives. Of course, I agree with him. Now allow me to show you the ladies parlor and then the one for the gentlemen."

They walked to the end of the lengthy corridor and faced two doors side by side; she opened the door on the left, and saw that Colette admired its décor as much as she had. "The opulent pink velvet draperies, the chaises covered in satin and silk floral with these colorful, Persian rugs are truly elegant. Didn't you say you had redecorating plans? Well I wouldn't change a thing in here, not even a single white rose."

"I arranged for the servants to keep fresh flowers in all the occupied rooms during the holidays. I know how much you enjoy them, even if they are from the indoor gardens. But of course this time of year where else might one find such beauty in nature?"

"Thank you dear Veronica, you are so thoughtful."

"You are quite welcome. Next to this is the men's parlor." Veronica opened the door to a room with oxblood leather seating, dark paneled walls, a few potted palm trees and large paintings of landscapes. "I believe this is where the men adjourn after supper to discuss world problems and probably puff smoke at each other. I am sure what they talk about would not interest us in the least."

"I am certain that is so," Colette laughed.

"Now we will have a look at the music room. The pianoforte has the most exquisite tone of any I've ever heard. And there is a very beautiful harp."

When they entered the room, Colette gazed at the harp. She rubbed her hand over the ram's head at the top and studied the gold trimmed, black polished wood. "I don't think I've ever seen a harp quite like this."

"This one has thirty-nine strings, and plays like the music of angels. Gavin bought it for Audrey on her fourteenth birthday from Sebastian Erad in London. Audrey is quite fond of it."

"I can see why, I hope she will play for us when she comes," Colette said trying out a few notes.

"Surely she would consider it an honor. Now I cannot wait for you to see the grand salon." Veronica led her through massive double doors which opened to a giant ballroom of gleaming, crystal chandeliers and a white marble floor.

"It's magnificent," Colette spoke in awe. "How many can this room hold?"

"About four hundred people, but Gavin said usually for our New Year's Eve ball there are only about three hundred that attend." Veronica pointed to the balcony above where the orchestra played. "We hire fifty musicians for the ball."

Colette sighed and opened her arms wide as if to embrace all that she saw. "I cannot get used the splendor of Ivywood. Aren't you overwhelmed with this estate? I know I would be. I had trouble getting used to Glenvalley and it is only half this grand."

"Indeed, I wake every morning mostly in utter disbelief that I am here, though just as often I say to myself that without Gavin it would be nothing. But we are only half finished with our tour, so we will move on to the library."

Again Colette was taken aback. "In spite of its size this room appears marvelously comfortable."

"It is, especially when the fireplace is glowing on these cold winter nights. There are over three thousand books in here," Veronica said perusing some of the titles. "Gavin insists that a servant be present when I use the ladder to go to the top. These ceilings are eighteen feet high and he is afraid that I might fall."

They moved on to the prodigiously large game room with its handsome mahogany billiard table, a dart board area, four tables for cards and a pair of long oxblood divans. There was also a carved mahogany counter at the far end from which food could be laid out.

Veronica started to chuckle. "Believe it or not, I have actually played a game of billiards with Gavin, and I nearly beat him. I know mother would say it was unladylike of me, but I enjoyed it and Gavin was highly amused. I think he was afraid I would beat him."

Colette laughed, "Perhaps with practice you could."

"Well enough of this, it will be time to eat soon and I want to show you the upstairs. Aside from the servants' quarters, the guest rooms throughout the third and forth floors can accommodate up to fifty visitors, including their personal maids and valets. However, most of the forth floor billets the housemaids, nursemaids and children's suites. In addition to the guest rooms on the third floor, there is our suite of rooms."

Colette enjoyed seeing Gavin and Veronica's stately bedroom, which was set between a private sitting room, bath, and dressing room for each of them. The master bedroom itself consisted of an oversized four-poster bed that sat high off the ground and was adorned with a canopy of red satin draperies. Accompanying the red throughout the room were accents of creamy white velvet and dark green damask. The furnishings were a mixture of tables and chests from China, floral paintings from France and in front of the enormous fireplace rested a white bear skin rug. Their suite, as well as most other rooms when occupied, hosted numerous fresh flowers in crystal and silver vases, along with palms and ferns of every sort and size in brass urns and painted pots.

"Now I'll show you the pantries and then lastly I want you to take a peak at the wine cellar," Veronica said. "Then we'll have some tea and dinner."

"I believed I would never see so much china and silver, and linen and lace as we have at Glenvalley," Colette declared when they had finished looking at the linen rooms and butlers' pantries. "You have outdone me sister."

"We do indeed have mounds of fine linen and a spectacular collection of elegant French porcelain and exquisite Meissen and Dresden from Germany. And truly I am quite fond of all the silver and crystal," Veronica proclaimed. "It all seems fit for a king. But enough of all these things; I wish I could show you the gardens. Above everything they are quite lovely but covered with snow. In the spring you will be most amazed by such beauty."

Chapter 7

Veronica and Colette headed for the wine vault. "Seeing this took me by surprise," Veronica said opening the heavy oak door.

"Are you sure you know your way around?" Colette asked, peering apprehensively into the dark. "I can't see much."

"Well, I have to admit that I've only been down here once before with Gavin. I should have brought a lantern, but never mind that, the candles will be enough. I think some of the wine is nearly as old as Methuselah, and there is—eeeeh!"

Veronica's shriek sent a chill through Colette. "What is it? What's the matter?" Colette screamed recoiling back a step with her sister.

"Did you see that hideous rat? I nearly fell over it," Veronica gasped feeling the bile rise in her throat as she was momentarily numbed with fear. "I think it ran under my skirt. Oh how I detest rodents! Never mind the wine cellar, let's get out of here."

She dashed to the top of the stairs ahead of Colette and leaned against the door to catch her breath. When she pulled at the door to open it, it would not move. "No, no, it can't be," she cried, the terror coming through in her voice.

"Is it locked, try it again!" Colette screamed, "How could it be locked?"

"I should have pulled on it rather than leaned on it."

"We're going to die down here with the rats." Colette paled and began banging on the door.

"Calm yourself sister and save your strength," Veronica admonished regaining a little composure. "No one can hear you through that piece of wood; it is not like a regular door."

"What will we do, what shall be done?" Colette entreated, her voice quivering.

"I just remembered that Gavin mentioned a window down here—ahh—!" Veronica shrieked again, her heart in her throat. "It's another rat." After being frozen in place for several moments, she forced herself to speak. "We must find that window, but there's no sign of outside light coming from anywhere. Oh! Now I remember!"

"What Veronica, tell me," Colette demanded, "Hurry."

"There is a door we have to go through before we're able to see the window. The door opens to a tunnel. I didn't actually see the door, but you must be brave and come with me. We'll find it together," Veronica declared.

"I can't move," Colette lamented. "I am petrified of another rat coming near me."

"Do you want to stay here alone, or are you going to follow me? Watch, let's swish our skirts around and make a lot of noise shuffling our feet, that should keep the varmints away." Veronica moved quickly down the stairs and onto the dirt floor of the cellar. "Now let's make haste and find that door."

"How do you know this will work?" Colette asked.

"Well," Veronica laughed for the first time. "Honestly, I don't; it just makes sense to me."

Reluctantly Colette agreed, and when she got to the bottom of the stairs she grabbed a tall stick that leaned up against the wall. "We can beat off those disgusting things with this." She started to giggle, thrashing the stick furiously on the ground around her. "We are a comic pair indeed, skipping and hopping about."

"Be careful not to drop your candle," Veronica cautioned, just as Colette saw another rat run past.

In her frenzy to get away from the pest she dropped the taper and broke it to pieces as she stepped backwards on it. "Oh now look what I've done," she moaned. "We better find that door post haste. You have only half a candle now and I'll surely die of fright if we end up in complete darkness. Perchance, our husbands will find us any minute."

"Well that's very possible if we have not surfaced within an hour or two. But one thing is certain; I will not be sitting in the dark waiting for them. I'm sure we can't be far from our tunnel door. Let's hurry," Veronica said as they began their dance steps and skirt swirls again.

While Veronica and Colette fretted in the wine cellar, Gavin and Basil played happily at billiards. "You seemed to have improved your game," Basil chuckled. "I used to be able to beat you more quickly than this."

Basil's bawdy laugh always caught Gavin off guard, *it does not seem to fit his gentlemanly countenance,* he thought. "You're joking of course, my boy." Gavin laughed heartily, negotiating the table to better his aim at the ball. "You have yet to best me at more than two games in a row in all your life. It does appear, however, that you might have honed your skills since we played last at Glenvalley; I noticed that last night. Actually you ought to let Veronica give you a lesson," he teased.

"Indeed. It's extraordinary. I am all amazement. She really put you to shame? You let her of course," Basil queried, studying the lay of the table with elaborate nonchalance, thinking how humiliated he would be if his sister-in-law were to beat him.

"Would you like me to arrange a game for the two of you?" Gavin asked, grinning to himself at the expression on Basil's face. "But, now that I think of it, I doubt that she'd show off her skill to you. She has said more than once that she would never play with anyone but me. You see, she's quite shy about it all."

Gavin smiled at Basil's small sigh of relief then changed the subject. "Say, I wonder what the girls are up to? Perhaps in an hour or so we should see to them, it will be time to eat in any case."

"That's a good idea. I'm a bit concerned about Colette, now that you mention it. It's been some time since they went off together."

"Indeed, it has," Gavin agreed. "It was directly after breakfast I believe. But then Veronica was quite excited about seeing Colette; she had a number of things to show her and talk about."

The two sisters went two thirds of the way around the enormous cavern before they found the door. With eyes accustomed to the dim candle light, Veronica tried to pull the portal open, but it barely moved. Refusing to be defeated, she took a deep breath.

"Stand back. I'm going to tug hard at this to see if it will open just enough for us to slip through."

With as much strength as she could muster, she jerked at the door, and without warning it swung wide open and threw Veronica into Colette; both landed on the floor.

"You poor dear, are you all right?" Veronica bent down to take her hand. "Let me help you up."

"I'm fine," Colette groused rubbing her backside. "Let's just get out of here and hope the rats don't follow."

They moved quicker than either believed possible, slammed the door shut and leaned against it panting for breath. "Oh no!" Veronica moaned. "Colette, I've lost my candle, all I have left is the holder. And where is your stick?"

"I can't believe I forgot to pick it up," she felt her stomach and brushed her blond hair from her face. "I see a hint of light at the end of the tunnel ahead. If it's the sun then I feel better already. I guess we can do without my stick and our tapers."

They reached the end of the passageway and came around the corner. "The window is so high," Veronica squinted, surveying the latch at the opening.

"And narrow," Colette fidgeted. "How shall we ever get through it?"

"Getting through might not be as difficult as getting it opened."

Veronica stared up at the cold light of day coming through. "It appears to be locked!"

"Oh Veronica how shall we ever get out, how can we reach the lock? I am sorry to whine; it is just that I'm tired and hungry. It seems I'm always this way since I have been increasing." Colette yawned, "What are we going to do?"

"I think if I can put my foot in your hand you can hoist me up, and I should be able to reach the lock."

Colette agreed and cupped her hand for Veronica's foot so she could reach the top of the window, but the latch would not move. "I know; I'll use the candle holder to knock it open. Can you help me up again?" Veronica asked.

"I'll try."

"It's snowing out," Veronica said as she tried to unlock the window with the large, silver candleholder. "Now look what I've done." She looked over the instrument's battered and bent shape. "It is clear we'll never use this again.

While holding Veronica up, Colette screamed as she felt something under her skirt. In a panic she let go of her sister. Veronica hung onto the window but with her weight pulling on it the entire window started to pull away from the wall. Then without warning, the heavy slate dropped to the ground and Veronica quickly rolled out of the way.

"Are you hurt?' Colette cried out reaching for Veronica's hand. "I am so sorry!"

"I'm fine, I think," she replied, and then started laughing and pointing to the fallen window casement; flattened beneath it lay the rat. "What a pair we make. As Father would say, sometimes we can be two of the silliest girls in the world."

When they finally stopped laughing, Colette felt better. "I refuse to allow some stupid rat to upset me again. I promise! It's time I started to be useful here." She helped her sister to her feet. "I have resolved to gather my strength. I must! I've been nothing but a burden to you throughout this entire ordeal. It is my turn to think of something, since you've done all the work thus far. Furthermore, I do not wish to spend the night down here."

Veronica spoke, feeling very tired as she rubbed her bruised shoulder. "It's clear that Gavin and Basil, if they are even looking, are not going to rescue us."

"I have an idea," Colette said, trying to boost her sister's spirits. "Cup your hands and lift me up by my foot and shove me out. Because I need the most help and you are lighter than I, I can pull you through the window easier than you can me."

Relieved that she did not have to do anymore thinking, Veronica smiled. "Your plan is good, thank you. Let's get started, and what are you giggling about?"

"I suddenly had a vision of Miss Phoebe and her sister down here. Mrs. Twackham is far too round and would never make it through the window."

Veronica conjured up the same picture, and all at once gales of laughter came forth from her and Colette. Neither could speak, until finally Veronica caught her breath.

"It must be our country upbringing and curiosity that caused us to even venture into this wine cellar in the first place," Veronica laughed. "I'm sure those two would consider it beneath them to look the place over."

After much ado and with Veronica's aid, Colette wiggled her way out of the opening onto the freezing snow. She lay on her protruding stomach and watched Veronica jump up several times in her endeavor to grab hold of the ledge. After much struggling, she finally caught Colette's hand. Soon after, though neither knew how, Veronica managed with all her strength to hoist herself up. They laughed so hard, tears streamed down their faces.

On their backs in the snow, the two girls were wrought-up with fatigue and did not feel the cold. Veronica lay there thinking, *I'll just close my eyes for a minute then we'll go inside.*

When she woke up, she was in bed with Gavin gazing down on her. "We were so worried about you and Colette," he said as he brushed her hair from her eyes and kissed her forehead. "The servants, Basil and I searched the mansion for you. We saw you outside from the cellar window; you were both unconscious. The doctor has been here. He said you could get up after you've rested, however, Colette must remain in bed until morning. How are you feeling?"

"I'm all right, just a little tired. You cannot know how glad I am to see you. We were a fright down there. After we crawled out that window, we were so exhausted that I thought we'd just rest for a minute and then go in. It's a good thing you came upon us."

"I can see that it has been quite an ordeal, I am so sorry for your trouble darling."

"Never mind that now, had you been looking for us long?"

"Just for as long as it took us to search the entirety of the manor, we even called out through the gardens until one of the servants suggested the Wine Cellar. Once we got down there we spotted the broken window and saw you lying on the ground outside, you can't imagine how quickly we moved. I thought Basil was going to come undone, and I was very much beside myself as well."

While Veronica and Gavin dined together in their room, he told her that, had she gone around the next corner of the tunnel, she would have found the door to the kitchen. He promised to bring her down there sometime soon so she could see, should they ever find themselves under such duress again.

"I assure you darling," Veronica said in all seriousness, "I have no intention of visiting the cellar again."

Chapter 8

On the second Friday in December Gavin's seventeen year old sister, Audrey, and their cousin Captain Douglas Bradford, arrived from the city of Bath. "It's wonderful to see you, dear brother, and Veronica, my sister." Audrey greeted them warmly, giving each a kiss on the cheek. "You both look very well."

"Indeed, married life suits you," Douglas Bradford agreed, looking smart even without his Captain's uniform. "It is good to have you back home from your travels." He turned and bowed to Basil and Colette. "And you are both well?"

"We are, thank you," Basil said returning his bow.

"Now, please before we go any further, allow me to introduce Mr. James Farnsworth of Bath," Douglas said, smiling broadly,

With her bold brown eyes Audrey stared up at the young, handsome Farnsworth, who towered over her and her cousin. "I'm indebted to Captain Bradford for affording me the opportunity to meet Miss Hunter's family," he said bowing to his new acquaintances.

"You are very welcome Mr. Farnsworth." Gavin smiled graciously.

"It's a pleasure to meet the one person Audrey wrote to us about while we were away."

"She's spoken a great deal of you both," Farnsworth said confidently, but inside he nervously weighted their reaction to his presence. "The captain too, has had many kind things to say about her brother's good fortune in securing your affections, my lady."

"My sister and cousin are quite right in that regard," Gavin chuckled, liking Farnsworth immediately, though he was eager to learn from his cousin what qualified him to be in his sisters company. "Now, I'm certain you three would like to refresh yourselves after your long journey."

"Indeed, you've been traveling all morning," Veronica agreed. "In about an hour I'll have Mrs. Anderson set out a light meal, and then later this evening we'll have a grand supper."

Veronica and Colette went upstairs to visit with Audrey while she settled in. "Dear sister," Audrey giggled, "what do you think of Mr. Farnsworth?"

"He's quite handsome, and I understand he has a substantial living," Veronica replied, thinking, *surely Audrey is completely in love with this self-assured young man.*

"His fortune means nothing to me. I think I would be just as fond of him if he lived on Doodlebug Road above a bookstore."

"Ah yes, my dear," Colette rejoined, "but perhaps if that were the case, your brother would not be too happy."

"Of course, you're right," Audrey sighed, pointing to the gowns she wanted her servant to take to the upstairs clothes room and which to leave out for the remainder of the day. "You know I am so glad we have the clothes room upstairs; to keep all these extra changes in the bedroom closets would be far too much crowding." She held up a blue velvet dress with lace at the neckline and asked, "Is this one lovely for supper Veronica?"

Veronica nodded her approval as Audrey continued. "I can assure you, my brother would never allow me to set foot outside of Ivywood under my cousin's care again if Mr. Farnsworth were a bookstore clerk. Nevertheless, James, I mean Mr. Farnsworth, told me that most of the young ladies he has been acquainted with were pretty much interested in his wealth more than him. He said he knew that his fortune was of little importance to me." She sighed as she handed her maid a white, velvet evening gown. "I'm so blessed to have my own sizeable living."

Veronica laughed, "Indeed you are my dear sister!"

"If I may inquire," Colette asked, "How long have you known Mr. Farnsworth now?"

"It's been almost as long as my brother and Veronica have been on their honeymoon. His mother is a friend of my aunt's where I stayed in Bath. Douglas introduced us one morning in the Pump room, as he was telling me about the baths. It was my first week there. Mr. Farnsworth came over to greet my cousin, and we were introduced. Right away I knew I liked him. And I could see in his eyes and his demeanor towards me that he liked me as well. Nearly every morning after that Mr. Farnsworth walked with Douglas and me around the Royal Crescent; it was perfect."

"He would be an excellent match for any proper young lady," Veronica said, as she got up to give Audrey a hug. "You have made a fine choice dear sister."

"Dearest Veronica," Audrey glowed, happy for her new sister's endorsement. "Now, don't you think it would be great fun to go ice skating this afternoon?"

"I'll speak to your brother about it while we're eating." Veronica turned to Colette, "What about you and Basil, would you enjoy such an outing?"

"It would be a nice change, though I'm not sure just how well I can skate in my condition."

"Oh, please come with us," Audrey pleaded. "I know cousin Douglas and Mr. Farnsworth want to skate. We talked about it on our journey here."

During their meal, everyone was thrilled at the suggestion of going to the pond, so Gavin whispered to the servant to have the sleighs brought around.

"Let's get started then; the ice is waiting." Gavin said motioning everyone to the door after they dressed for the cold outdoors. "The sleighs are waiting for us."

"I think the temperature has dropped considerably," Veronica said stepping into the sleigh with Gavin's help. "I'm glad it is only a five minute ride."

Gavin tucked one of the wool blankets closely around his wife. "I believe it started to snow as soon as the three of you arrived."

When they reached the pond Audrey and James crossed to the far side. Basil and Colette skated together, while Douglas Bradford went around the ice with Veronica and Gavin.

"Douglas, we're so happy you could join us this year," Gavin said holding Veronica's arm. "It is apparent that my sister is quite taken with this Farnsworth fellow. What can you tell me about his character; I trust you have inquired after his moral fiber? But of course, you would not forgo such a necessary detail."

"Surely Gavin, do you think me a dunce?" Douglas smiled wrapping his red wool scarf more closely under his chin. "I would never allow dearest Audrey to associate with any one other than a gentleman superior in character and worth. I've known Farnsworth these past three years; he comes from one of the finest families in Bath, and he is a very steady fellow. You will also be pleased to know that of the many young gentlemen who wished to endear themselves to your sister, I have been loath to allow any such attachments until this one." Douglas looked out across the pond and sighed. "How I admire young love. Just watching Audrey and Farnsworth together brings back memories that are now becoming a blur."

Captain Bradford did not command an imposing presence, but his countenance bespoke gentleness, and women liked that about him. He had once loved a young lady who died two months before they were to be married. That was five years earlier, and since then he had not found anyone to whom he wanted to give his heart.

"Oh, Captain Bradford," Veronica said tenderly, "Gavin told me of the pain you endured over your lost love. I'm sorry to remind you of it, but you still have your youth. Someday you will have the same true love again. I'm certain of it."

"To be sure," Gavin added.

"Perhaps you are right," Douglas agreed, "perhaps someday."

James Farnsworth and Douglas Bradford had spent many evenings over the past six months talking about Audrey and her brother. The day before they left for Ivywood, James had confided in Douglas that he planned to propose to Audrey as soon as he met her family. As the two love birds skated together in silence, James gazed down at her, admiring her full rosy cheeks and the soft dark curls that framed her sweet face.

Suddenly he felt nervous but determined. "Miss Hunter," he stammered in tense anticipation. "Audrey, may I speak boldly? Nay, I'm compelled to confess what you must certainly already know. Since meeting you this summer, I have believed you are the loveliest young lady of my acquaintance. Please forgive me for being forthright, but because I love you so very much, I cannot waste another moment while we have this time by ourselves. I want you to be my wife; will you marry me dearest, beautiful Audrey?"

She looked up at him, her eyes gleefully twinkling, and her voice lively and spirited. "Oh yes, Mr. Farnsworth. I cannot help but be brave as well, though I believe it is proper for a young lady to be coy and perhaps decline when she receives her first proposal. Nevertheless, I'll not allow you to think that I must consider my answer. In truth, I do love you James. You have made me very happy by asking me to be your wife."

"Lovely Audrey, I want to kiss you right now, but I fear everyone is watching us, so I will have to endure a little longer. I shall speak to your brother directly." The rush of color that came over Audrey gratified him. "I am so glad you're pleased."

He beamed fondly at her and then guided her towards her brother. After a few polite words, Farnsworth took Gavin aside and nervously, but with fortitude, asked permission for his sister's hand.

All hugs and kisses in the sleigh ride home, no one was surprised to hear the news of James and Audrey's engagement. At supper

Gavin was pleased to toast his future brother-in-law and announced that James and Audrey would be married a year from the coming spring.

Late in the afternoon the next day, Veronica's parents arrived with her unmarried sisters, Louisa nineteen, and Harriet eighteen. Almost immediately, Veronica noticed the difference in Harriet and Louisa that Colette had told her about. Veronica had always considered Louisa pretty, but now she seemed almost beautiful. While Harriet did not have the same fine features as her sister, she looked very attractive with her new hairstyle pulled back off her face. Indeed, both Harriet and Louisa had definitely improved their countenance and manners.

Gavin was pleasantly surprised to see the transformation in Louisa and Harriet as well. "I quite agree with you regarding the change in your younger sisters," he said holding Veronica close as they sat before the roaring fire in their bedroom later that evening. "Whatever transpired between them while we were gone has made a difference. I feel certain they will secure the affections of one of our acquaintances at our New Year's Eve Ball."

"I know mother would be pleased if such a thing happened. Notwithstanding," Veronica chuckled straightening her white satin robe and gown. "There seems to be no change in her, as her verbosity remains the same."

"She does carry on a bit about how she believes your sisters will marry well because of my connections." Gavin took Veronica's hands in his and held them close to his chest, hoping to warm them for her.

"Well," Veronica laughed. "What's a daughter to do with a mother like mine?"

"Not a thing, not a thing. She's amusing just as she is and if not for her to entertain us, who should do as good a job," he chuckled, "except perhaps Miss Phoebe and her sister, Mrs. Twackham?"

"I believe you're right, and we will find out soon enough. They are due sometime tomorrow the post said."

"I'm glad for Basil's sake that they are coming, but I could do without seeing his odious sisters." He stood up and lifted Veronica to his side. "Now definitely on a more pleasant note, would you like to warm up under the luxury of our wonderful down quilts?"

With butterflies in her stomach at the expectation of his arms enfolding her, Veronica demurely walked beside him to the comfort of their bed.

When Miss Phoebe arrived with her sister Ursula and her husband Mr. Twackham, everyone was delighted to meet Mr. Twackham's twenty-eight-year-old bachelor cousin, David Tristam. Louisa and Harriet talked with Veronica about him in their bedroom as they prepared for bed.

"I understand from Colette," Louisa said with interest as she slipped into her pink, muslin nightgown, "that Mr. Tristam's been in the East Indies for the past several years. He's really quite dashing, isn't he?"

"He is indeed," Veronica said, pleased with her sisters' improvements to their conduct and appearance, "And he is well traveled, or so I've heard. And now that you both have learned to be proper young ladies, you should be in excellent form to appease Mother's worries and become acquainted with some eligible gentlemen while you're here. I'm so proud of you."

"Well, I don't know about Louisa, but a clergyman would suit me perfectly." Harriet sighed as she brushed her long, straight auburn hair. "Colette told me Mr. Tristam has a fortune of fifteen thousand a year from the trade, and he stands to inherit another ten when his aunt dies!"

"I imagine women of all ages pursue him for his wealth and connections," Veronica commented. "While it would be nice if you both were able to secure the affection of a wealthy young bachelor like Mr. Tristam, I sincerely hope, dear sisters that you will marry for love."

"It is the only way," Louisa sighed. "However, that does not mean I cannot admire a gentleman like Mr. Tristam. He is certainly very good looking," she said, remembering his smile when they were introduced. "But I imagine someone like him with so much money is quite indifferent to a pretty face. And I am sure, Harriet, that he would never find the likes of you or I of any interest. Indeed we shall have to settle for a man in uniform and pray that true love abounds."

"Don't be too certain of your opinion," Harriet admonished. "As pretty as you are Louisa, and with your accomplishments you would please many men, regardless of their station in life."

"Say what you will," Louisa said, climbing into her bed. "I could never believe a man as charming and rich as Mr. Tristam would be interested in someone with my lack of connection or fortune. An officer will do for me."

"I think it is time to say goodnight, it's late," Veronica yawned and got up to kiss her sisters. "It is wonderful to have you here."

Following Phoebe, Mr. Tristam and the Twackhams' arrival were Mr. and Mrs. Gerard, neighbors of the Stuarts'. They brought with them their only child, Sarah Grace, who could often be heard complaining about having to wait until she was seventeen before being allowed to attend a ball.

"Sarah Grace," Harriet Stuart consoled her with her self-imposed wisdom, "your mother and father are wise to keep you from attending a ball until you are of age; after all, you'll be seventeen in March and that is only three months away. As our sister Gabriella is proof, we may acknowledge that being out too young can cause irreversible damage to a young lady, good sense or not."

"Of course you're right," Sarah Grace replied, letting down her lustrous black hair. "I am so glad you are here to help me settle in. I did promise Mama and Papa not to grumble about not going to the Hunter's New Year's Eve ball. However, I will be permitted to observe it with Miss Bischone by my side, but then we must return to my room by midnight."

"How do you like your new governess? Miss Bischone seems very strict I think," Harriet said, admiring Sarah's long natural curls. "I hardly see you anymore since she arrived two months ago."

"Mother says she's to see to it that I become a proper young lady, fit to come out into society and attend my first ball. Miss Bischone is worse than Miss Brown ever was. I never thought anyone could be as stern as her," Sarah giggled. "I certainly hope I don't end up an old maid like my governesses; that would be dreadful indeed."

"I don't think there's any chance of that happening," Harriet laughed. "You are even more beautiful than any of my sisters, and they are all considered beauties."

Chapter 9

A fortnight prior to Christmas Day Gavin received an astonishing post from his cousin, Lillian Ramsay. She related that on their way to the South of France, her mother, Lady Ramsay, having been in such an anxious and agitated state over the appearance of her stepson, had died of heart failure. It happened just outside of London where Lillian had the foresight to send a servant to fetch her half-brother, Edward Ramsay.

"But how shall we find Mr. Ramsay in London, Miss?" the servants questioned when Lillian ordered them to bring him to her.

"Here's his address. He gave it to me just before my mother, God rest her soul, demanded that he leave our home." Lillian spoke with a resolve and firm tone that none of the servants at the Ramsay estate had ever heard coming from her. "Hurry now and don't come back without him. Here is a brief note I've written asking for his help."

About ten miles south of London, Lillian and her mother had taken rooms at the Knight's Bridge Inn because Lady Ramsay had complained of feeling poorly. Lillian had thought that if her mother could rest for a few days before going on to Dover and then to France she would feel better; but her mother had died in her sleep their first night at the inn. When the crying servant came to wake Lillian and tell her of the tragedy, Lillian was stunned. She went to see her mother and for about an hour she'd knelt by her bedside and wept. When she returned to her room, she wrote the note to Edward.

The next morning while she waited for him to arrive, she dismissed her nurse Jessica. "I promise you Jessie, I will be fine. Your services are no longer needed. We will send your things to whatever address you like, and I will include six months wages. George can take you to London; I know you have a sister there."

Lillian then turned to her personal maid, Maureen. "I won't need you again until after my brother comes. Then I'll call for you."

"But Miss Lillian, you cannot really mean..."

"I mean exactly that Maureen. Now be off, and do not disturb me until I send Oliver for you. I want some time alone, is that understood?"

"Yes my lady," Maureen stammered. "It has been twenty years since I left your side; how shall I bear it?"

"You needn't worry dear," Lillian said gently. "It's just that I am determined to change my life. Furthermore, I feel better than I've ever felt before. For as long as I can remember, I've been sickly, and I'll have no more of it."

"I'm very glad to hear it Miss Lillian. That relieves my mind some. But should you have need of me, I won't be far away."

Upon Edward's arrival at the Inn he was astounded to find Lillian completely altered. "Dear sister, I expected to see you weeping and beside yourself. Instead, to my amazement, you look perfectly wonderful; your complexion is radiant."

"I'm overjoyed to see you Edward. Thank you for coming. As I said in my letter, I hope you won't mind helping with the arrangements for the funeral at Lochaven. First, though before you say another word, please accept my apologies for my mother's behavior toward you."

"I was so pleased to know that you did not feel the same about my coming home as she did. Indeed, I am quite gratified that you asked for my help. Rest assured, I will see to everything."

To his surprise upon telling her this, she ran into his arms and sobbed. "Oh Edward, I am exceedingly obliged to you. While I'm sorry for my mother's passing, I cry because of your kindness and friendship. Your coming to help gives me great joy. And though I'm sure my mother meant well, I have been overshadowed by her domineering nature for too long now." Tears streamed down her cheeks. "How odd it is that I should experience such feelings of relief and well-being. Thank you Edward."

"It's to be expected to some extent, dear sister. I can understand that you have a sense of relief, or should I say freedom. Nonetheless, we needn't discuss the matter."

They proceeded to Lochaven the next day and buried Lady Ramsay in a private service. Lillian did not wish to feign sadness, when she sensed liberation, nor did she want staring eyes expecting her to be tearful. Her post to the Hunters conveyed that she and Edward would be arriving at Ivywood the Monday before Christmas. The Hunters were not informed of any more than what the post had made clear. It read:

....You are not to concern yourselves about the details, or the funeral arrangements. Everything has been done that can be done. We will tell you all upon our arrival. And indeed, my new brother, Edward, is quite anxious to make your acquaintance.

Fondly, Lillian Ramsay

Gavin and Veronica were early risers, and most mornings before leaving the comfort of their cozy quilts the two often discussed family matters. "I'm quite pleased to see that Audrey is so happily betrothed," Gavin said, loosening his bed jacket from the warmth of their roaring fire.

"Yes, indeed, and to such as fine a gentleman as Mr. Farnsworth," Veronica replied, as she stretched out her arms and ran her fingers through her mussed hair. "I imagine there will be many broken hearts, or at least a few pocketbooks pining over the loss of your sister's inheritance when we announce her engagement at our New Year's Eve Ball."

"Clearly that is so, even if only through the Hunter name, as my sister hardly knows any of the young men around here or in London. Yet, of course, they know of her and her fortune. There is no doubt, however, that in Bath there will definitely be young men in mourning. Thank goodness she was in my cousin's care while we were gone."

"I'll inform Mrs. Anderson today that after the Twelfth Night Celebrations, preparations for Audrey's engagement party in May need to begin."

"And," Gavin said, "I'll let our steward, Mr. Walton, know. Between him and the housekeeper it should be an excellent affair."

"I'm so glad Mrs. Anderson is here to help with things like this," Veronica said. "Indeed, I am relieved that I do not have to tackle the job alone. I'm afraid, I might be at a loss to carry off such a show as is necessary for the kind of gathering we'll have for Audrey and Mr. Farnsworth."

"I noticed that Mrs. Anderson has done a splendid job of keeping Miss Phoebe and her sister away from us and the Vances during meals." Gavin laughed, "But I can't help wondering, does it appear that perhaps Miss Phoebe is more civil towards you?"

Veronica leaned on her elbow and smiled. "I believe it's just a disguise she wears for her brother's sake. Unmistakably, she still displays a haughty attitude, and I am quite uncomfortable just carrying on a polite conversation with her."

Gavin took her hand in his. "Well, I should imagine that you have little to say to each other anyway, except for the common greetings such as good morning and good evening."

"This is true," Veronica began to giggle, "Her conceit is equal only to her lack of character and the size of her disagreeably, large nose."

"She certainly does not have the sweet nature of her brother. Indeed, she and her sister's behavior are similarly disappointing." Gavin kissed his bride on the cheek. "I believe it is time for me to dress. I'm taking our guests shooting this morning. We will return before Lillian and Mr. Ramsay arrive."

Veronica loved the smell of burning wood and the warmth coming from her fireplace as she did her morning devotions—reading the Bible, saying prayers and sometimes writing or answering letters. Afterwards, she enjoyed having Margaret help her prepare for the day ahead, doing her hair and setting out her morning clothes.

"Are you pleased to have family here, my lady?" Margaret asked as she put the finishing touches on Veronica's coiffure.

"I can't tell you how much. I missed them a little while we were on our honeymoon," she replied, looking towards her door. "I think my sister is here."

"Have you time for a visit?" Colette asked, peaking in as Margaret opened the door.

"Of course, come in. It will be good to have some time together before we go down to breakfast with the other ladies. I take it the hunting party has left for the morning?"

"Oh yes, about thirty minutes ago," Colette smiled prettily with her blond curls set softly around her handsome face.

"Gavin said goodbye just before I stepped into the bath. I've been anxious to talk with you about Louisa and Harriet. I am so proud of them; they've truly become very agreeable young ladies."

"I am pleased too," Colette said, checking her hair in the mirror as she stood behind Veronica. "Now they seem quite fit to keep the same company we do, don't you think?"

"Indeed, they have poise and manners I never thought possible for our once silly sisters. Their tutors did an excellent job in advising them on dress and comportment." Veronica turned so Margaret could finish buttoning the back of her blue gown for her. "Louisa has always held a certain innocent beauty with her delicate curls framing her pretty face. And I'm proud of Harriet too. Though she is less favored with the beauty Louisa and Gabriella possess, she has done quite well with what she has. Her hair, straight as it is, looks very attractive pulled back off her face."

Colette laughed. "I'm glad she finally gave up trying to curl it. I was tired of seeing it fall in her face all the time."

Veronica sighed and then smiled broadly. "I've noticed our tall

74

amiable vicar seems to favor Harriet. He would be a good match for her. I am eager to see if he will stop by again today as he has for the past four. Since Gavin and I have been home from our honeymoon we see him only on Sundays or when we invite him for dinner."

"Well it's interesting to watch them," Colette grinned, "but I am anxious also to see what transpires between Louisa and Mr. David Tristam this afternoon. I saw him walk over and sit by her twice yesterday and once the day before. She seems quite flustered by his attentions, but I dare say there is some interest on his part."

"I believe there is, and I can't say that I'm surprised. Her voice is absolutely stunning. I have watched the last two nights when she sings and while Miss Phoebe frowns, I'm certain out of jealousy for Louisa's performances, Mr. Tristam cannot seem to keep his eyes off Louisa."

"Why do you laugh?" Colette asked.

"I was just thinking how gratifying it would be if another relative of Miss Phoebe's should fall in love with a Stuart."

"I quite agree."

Veronica stood up to head downstairs. "Shall we face the odious Vance sisters together?"

"Yes, I'm ready. Truly, we should not leave poor Harriet and Louisa by themselves with those two," Colette laughed. "Veronica, are you and Gavin looking forward to meeting his new cousin today?"

"We are, and I am even more zealous to see Lillian. We received a post from Rosemary yesterday saying that we will not recognize her."

Chapter 10

When Lillian Ramsay and her half-brother Edward arrived at Ivywood, they did not know her as the frail, unhealthy girl from Lochaven. She astonished everyone because of the change in her— she looked quite altered and was even pretty.

"Lillian, you are very welcome to Ivywood," Gavin bent to kiss her check. "You look well, dear cousin."

Veronica took her hand. "We were sorry indeed, to hear about Lady Ramsay."

Lillian smiled as Gavin had never seen before. "Thank you for your warm salutations and sincere condolence. But now, please allow me to introduce Mr. Edward Ramsay, recently from America. Without him I could not have managed. Edward, Miss Audrey Hunter and her brother, Gavin, and this is his lovely bride Veronica, and Gavin's cousin, Captain Douglas Bradford."

"And may I have the pleasure of introducing Mr. James Farnsworth," Gavin gestured for Farnsworth to step forward, "my sister's fiancé."

A broad smile crossed Lillian's face. "Audrey, my darling cousin, I see that best wishes are in order." She leaned toward her and whispered, "You must tell me all about this later."

Edward Ramsay started to put his hand out, but after a moment he bowed as the others had. "I'm delighted to meet each of you. And all sadness aside for the ill fate of my dearly beloved stepmother, God rest her soul, it pleases me more than words can say to be able to celebrate the holidays with you." Edward spoke in his smooth, charming accent that clearly was not English.

As he was introduced to Phoebe Vance, she nearly swooned when his tall blond headed stature bowed to her. With obvious excitement she curtsied, feeling certain that destiny had brought Mr. Ramsay to Ivywood solely for her benefit. The tone of his unduly irresistible manner of speech, coupled with his fine yellow curls and bold blue eyes, wholly possessed Miss Phoebe's simple-mindedness. She was completely imperceptive to the fact that every woman he'd ever met fell in love first with his money, and then with the gracious luxury in which he treated everyone.

Notwithstanding the glorious appearance of an eligible bachelor for the self appointed Phoebe, Lillian Ramsay's transformation took Captain Douglas Bradford completely by surprise. "What a wonderful thing it is to see you looking so well, Lillian." He bowed, awed by her once undernourished figure, which now appeared almost voluptuous; additionally, her countenance and rosy cheeks had been transformed from their sad, ghost-like condition.

Lillian curtsied, her blue eyes shining brightly behind long curled lashes. "It's good to see you too, Douglas."

He smiled handsomely at her and admired her luminous blond tresses. *Even her proper black mourning attire does her great justice. Indeed, I'm quite charmed,* he thought.

By the time Christmas Eve day settled upon Ivywood and its guests, it was evident that the vicar, John Boswell, had taken a fancy to Harriet Stuart. Mr. Boswell, the youngest son of an earl, some thought, did not have much to recommend him. Primarily, his inclination to the ministry and his contentment with the simple life the countryside afforded him was a drawback to most young ladies. Moreover, his mere living of five hundred a year made him undesirable to those who wanted more out of life than his dreary income could afford. These things, however, did not concern John Boswell or Harriet Stuart.

After his second evening with the Hunters and their guests, he had been quite pleased to receive an open invitation to Ivywood. "Please Boswell," Gavin had said, "during these happy holidays feel free to drop by for a meal whenever you like. I'm certain our family and friends would be delighted for your company."

John had replied that he would like that very much, and he had not missed a day since. He enjoyed most conversing with Harriet. It was the only time in his adult life at age twenty-seven that he had met a young lady with whom he felt he had a great deal in common.

"You do such a nice job on my new hair style Alice," Harriet said gazing into the mirror with a smile. "I think this is the first Twelfth Night Holiday I have enjoyed myself so completely; indeed, it has turned out to be a wonderful holiday season."

"It does seem, Miss Harriet, that when one is having a good time it gets away from us faster than we like." Though she was heavy set, Alice's fingers were nimble and she did Harriet and Louisa's hair quickly and with precision.

"You're so right. And Alice, I know I can trust you not to repeat what I tell you in confidence, but I wanted to share my joy with you."

"I am honored by your trust, and you may be assured of my silence. But if you will allow me the liberty, I think I can guess what, I mean who, is the cause of your happiness. Is it not due to the attentions of a certain gentleman who you mentioned the other day? And is he still showing you great favor?"

"Yes, and Mr. Boswell is his name. I'm pleased to say that he shares the same love of Christian enlightenment and books that I do. I have dreamt often of meeting someone like him."

"I'm very happy for you," Alice said as she applied a light touch of rouge to Harriet's cheeks. "You know, you are very pretty when you smile, but this wee bit of color will enhance your beauty. And may I ask is the gentleman you refer to handsome?"

"I think so. He has dark hair and sincere brown eyes, but what I like most about his appearance is his smile. However, more important than his good looks is his wonderful sense of humor; he even makes me laugh."

"Is that so hard to do?" Alice asked, putting the finishing touches on her hair. "But now I wanted you to know that I have heard many glad tidings of your brother-in-law, Mr. Hunter. The servants here have nothing but good to say about the Master and his generosity."

"What is it Alice? I think I should like to hear. They will only confirm what I already believe is true about my dear sister's husband."

Alice smiled. "The word is that the Hunters and their guests will be caroling tonight. Everyone says how they've never seen anything like the kindness they've received from the newlyweds of Ivywood. They say the Hunters took time just before their holiday guests arrived to hand out new blankets, bolts of material and food baskets to all their tenants and servants. Your sister and brother-in-law are determined to see that no one lacks while they have plenty. That's what the cooks are all talking about in the kitchen."

Harriet stood up to go downstairs. "Thank you Alice for telling me, but now I'll be off to join the others for breakfast."

Much to Harriet's disappointment, most of that day was spent anxiously waiting for Mr. Boswell to appear. Not until three in the afternoon did he send word that he would be unable to visit Ivywood until it came time for caroling. Now as everyone waited for the sleighs to be brought around, she thought she saw him coming toward her. Her heart beat so fast that she had difficulty remaining calm; but when she lost sight of him, she suddenly had misgivings. *What if he doesn't try to sit with to me?*

"Miss Harriet, may I help you up?" Boswell asked, startling her from behind. "Perhaps between us we can keep the cold away," he chuckled as she stepped into the sleigh.

"Why, Mr. Boswell, thank you," she replied with the touch of his hand on her waist sending a sweet chill down her spine.

It did not escape Mrs. Stuart's notice that John Boswell had a keen interest in their youngest daughter. "Mr. Stuart," she said nudging her husband in his ribs, "Didn't I tell you he would be here. And did you see? He could not wait to procure a seat next to Harriet."

Annoyed by his verbose wife's incessant poking in his ribs, he replied in a whisper, "Of course, madam, I am not blind. However, I will have to wrap my ribs if you don't stop prodding me with your elbow."

Twenty-six year old Phoebe Vance was not as fortunate in matters of the heart as some of the other young ladies. Over the years a long line of disinterested bachelors had dashed her expectations for a husband. Then when she had failed to capture the affections of Gavin Hunter she had lost hope, especially when she saw that he favored someone without fortune or connections. Moreover, in spite of Phoebe's want of veracity and good judgment, she could not help but notice that two of the Stuart sisters had fared far better than she in their conquests. This primarily came to light when she observed David Tristam's partiality towards Louisa Stuart.

Forthwith, Phoebe was forced to consider her own wealth of fifty thousand pounds and wonder why she had been unable to secure a husband. She did not like the vision of herself as an old maid. With this in mind she felt certain that Mr. Edward Ramsay had been placed in her path for matrimony. Even though any hint of affection on his part had not as yet become noticeable, she possessed high hopes of success, and had every intention of obtaining a seat next to him for their caroling.

Albeit, she was quite disappointed when rather than sit next to Edward, she had to be satisfied with being down and across from him. *To think,* she thought, *that I should endure being pressed next to the taciturn David Tristam. I must remember to tell my sister later of this regrettable situation—that Louisa Stuart managed to find a seat between Mr. Ramsay and Captain Bradford, and I have to sit across from that insipid Lillian Ramsay. I'm not in the least amused.* With these less than endearing thoughts, a frown remained on Phoebe's sour face throughout most of the caroling, but no one bothered with her, so it mattered little.

David Tristam was not displeased about sitting across from rather than next to Louisa Stuart. *The better to admire her* he thought. Many times since the day they met he had spent wonderful hours telling her about his travels. *She seems so interested in my stories, she plays a fair hand of whist, and when we parlor dance she is a delightful partner. Above all, though, I think I admire her stunning operatic solos the most.* He found himself waking up the past several mornings thinking about the prospect of Louisa's singing after supper, as she had done nearly every night since they arrived. *Her pleasing countenance exudes an innocent vitality that I find quite unique. Indeed, I see few of these attributes in most women I know, and Louisa's naïveté fascinates me.*

"Miss Louisa," he addressed her once they got underway in the sleighs, "I trust after caroling in the cold night air that you will still be able to entertain us later this evening with one of your beautiful melodies."

"Have no fear Mr. Tristam, I will be fine. Thank you for your concern though. I'm certain each of the young ladies present will enjoy offering music to those who care to listen. Isn't that right Miss Lillian," she smiled at her new friend.

Lillian laughed, snuggling her hands further into her white fur muff. "Perhaps you don't know that my piano playing needs practice and as for singing, I'll leave that to you and the others. What about you Miss Phoebe, shall you play for us as well?"

"I'll be happy to take my turn," Phoebe replied curtly.

"I believe all of the young ladies here at Ivywood have wonderful talents," Edward Ramsay said, annoyed by Phoebe's tart reply. For the remainder of the ride no one paid much attention to her.

Chapter 11

After caroling and changing into their evening gowns, Louisa, Harriet, Audrey and Lillian had agreed to meet in Lillian's room. As they waited for Lillian's maid to finish putting her blond tresses in order a broad grin crossed Audrey's face.

"Lillian," she spoke boldly, "It appears that Captain Bradford favors your company a great deal."

"I believe there are several attachments in the making this holiday." Harriet sighed, reveling at the thought of the vicar paying her a great deal of attention, though she did not dare speak of it.

Lillian laughed pointing to a curl that was out of place. "I think you may be right Miss Harriet, but it would be highly improper for me to consider anyone's favors, as I am in a state of mourning. Nonetheless, I sincerely believe the Vicar of Ivywood is quite fond of you."

Everyone laughed except Harriet; she blushed and didn't know what to say. Of course, she wanted Lillian's remarks about Mr. Boswell to be true, but she feigned ignorance. "I think not," she replied.

"Really, Harriet, Miss Lillian is right," Louisa insisted. "The vicar does prefer you to anyone else when he's here. I overheard Mr. Hunter say that Mr. Boswell has paid more visits to Ivywood in the past three weeks than in the entire year."

"I don't know about Mr. Boswell," Harriet said guardedly, hiding her discomfort, "but I believe Miss Phoebe will be quite put out that Mr. Twackham's cousin favors you Louisa."

"Indeed," said Audrey with glee that was unlike her. "It would serve Miss Phoebe right for all of us to marry ahead of her, inasmuch as I disliked her when she was after my brother. It was obvious to everyone that he was in love with Veronica."

Louisa laughed scornfully. "Really, it would be such equity if she were to marry a military man. She clearly thought herself above associating with us as well as the militia when they came to town last year. As for Mr. David Tristam, I don't know," she said awkwardly, yet relishing thoughts of his attentiveness towards her since his arrival. "I have not suspected that there is any partiality on his part."

"Then you truly need spectacles dear Louisa," Harriet laughed. "You may find it difficult to believe that a gentleman of Mr. Tristam's standing in society could be interested in you, nevertheless, I believe he is."

Louisa did not respond immediately, but finally she allowed, "It's true that I do enjoy his attentions. And surely he is very good looking with his wavy auburn hair and green eyes. But perhaps he simply appreciates having someone to listen to his adventure stories. He is clearly a man of great valor and wisdom I think."

Just then Veronica and Colette knocked on the door and peeked in. "May we come in?" Veronica asked.

"Where is Miss Phoebe?" Colette inquired looking around the room.

"She's with her sister," Audrey answered, gesturing for them to come in and close the door. "We invited her to join us, but she said she needed to see Mrs. Twackham for something."

Colette smiled, "Well, we did not stop by to spy on you but to let you know dinner will be served in half an hour. We'll see you downstairs then."

"I must tell you," Veronica said to Colette on the way to the drawing room, "Miss Phoebe does seem to put on a show of being a bit more civil and less odious since we last saw each other at the wedding. Gavin asked me if I thought she had changed. I had to admit then that I did not think so, though in front of others she can be amiable in an arrogant way."

"I would not trust her," Colette said.

"Indeed, I do not. I feel sorry for you dear, having to endure such a sister-in-law. She owns very little rectitude, a fact which is apparent even to the undiscerning eye." Veronica laughed, "We are fortunate that at present she is occupied with the pursuit of securing Mr. Ramsay's affections."

Colette laughed as well. "And for her occupation of it I'm grateful."

While Miss Phoebe's maidservant put the finishing touches to Phoebe's coarse, blond hair, she and Mrs. Twackham discussed the Stuart sisters. "Dear Phoebe," Ursula said while trying to repose her round figure on a blue velvet chaise, whose width was only half as wide as hers. "I do not see how it is possible and perhaps I'm wrong, I certainly hope so, that my husband's cousin, Mr. Tristam, could have any interest in one such as Louisa Stuart. Imagine, him falling for someone like her. She is without fortune and has absolutely no connections."

"Indeed, I am as astonished as you sister," Phoebe proclaimed disdainfully. "But let's pray that we are both incorrect in our perceptions. We must only hope that it cannot possibly be so, for in addition to her lack of distinction, I find Miss Louisa wanting in poise and accomplishment; though I will admit she can sing better than her sisters. Aside from that she is dull and has nothing to recommend her to a handsome, wealthy gentleman like your cousin."

"Mr. Twackham and I had hoped his cousin would take a fancy to you."

"I am sorry to admit that Mr. David Tristam favors Miss Louisa," Phoebe said. "I'm quite beside myself thinking he might have such poor judgment. To think of another Stuart sister as a possible relative is more than I can bear. And it is sad indeed, that Mr. Hunter had the misfortune to choose Veronica Stuart for his wife, when he could have had me for the asking. I'm quite disappointed in him."

"Well perchance to overcome our setback, we can continue in our expectations of the dashing Mr. Ramsay," Ursula suggested, twisting her short body to get comfortable.

"Certainly his wealth is equal to his other admirable qualities." Phoebe brightened at the thought, "To secure his affections would be in his best interest as well as mine. It may even be that I was overlooked by Mr. Hunter precisely to enable me to form an attachment with this handsome new addition to our company." She took one more look in the mirror at her straw like hair and sighed, "Well I'm ready Ursula. Do you think that I look well enough to appeal to Mr. Ramsay?"

"Of course dear, how could he resist?" Ursula spoke with self assuredness, lacking as much perspicacity as her homely sister was deficient in beauty and charm. "With such a figure as yours, I'm quite envious. I should be as trim."

Ursula grunted a little as she tried to heave herself from the narrow chaise. She and her husband were both short and fat, but his obesity came from excessive indulgence in alcoholic beverages, hers was from overeating. Therefore, with great effort in an attempt to keep her corpulent body upright, she tripped over her pudgy feet and fell back into the seat. It could not sustain the heavy thud of her mass, and two of the chaise's back legs broke in half. With a surprised look on her fleshy face she fell to the floor.

Phoebe jumped to her sister's aid and bid the servant to help her hoist Ursula off the rug. "Are you hurt my dear?" Phoebe asked. "Oh my look what we've done. Surely this settee must have been quite old." Phoebe waved for the servant to clean up the mess and without further ado said to Ursula, "Shall we go?"

Ursula, whose height reached only as high as her sister's undistinguished bosom, hobbled for a minute. But soon she was able to take Phoebe's arm leaving the other hand free to rub her backside as they walked down the hall. The servant, one of several who lacked respect much less affection for the sisters, stifled her laughter at Ursula's misfortune until she closed the door behind them.

For Christmas Eve Supper the grand dining salon overflowed with pine boughs and holly, and a lavishly appointed table. David Tristam sat next to Louisa, as he had for the past fortnight.

"Miss Louisa," he said admiring her hourglass figure and pretty face, "I must entreat you to do us the honor of being the first to sing this evening. It seems that throughout the day your melodies ring over and over in my head."

The color rose high in her cheeks at his compliment. "Why sir, you are bold and full of high praise. But surely Mr. Tristam, to hear me sing is of little consequence. It is much more pleasant to learn of your travels. After all, many can sing, but few have had the vast experience and knowledge of the world as you. I would much prefer for you to tell me about India or the Nile, as I'll probably never see the world I've read about. I will just have to settle for the hearing of it."

"Alas," he sighed, not thinking of travel but rather of the mystery of Louisa's unaffected simplicity and beauty. "No matter how exciting it is to travel, I have been away from England too long. It is a pleasure to know that there are a few like yourself Miss Louisa, whose enthusiasm for a world beyond your own impresses me greatly. To be able to share my travels with someone who enjoys hearing about them is a great pleasure indeed. As to preferring my stories to your singing, you are most definitely in error. However, since you ask, it would please me to share my adventures with you whenever you like. Truly I have met few young ladies who have any interest at all."

"Please sir, don't tease me, for I could never tire of your stories. I do not see how anyone could."

Since Lillian Ramsay arrived, she and Captain Bradford found themselves engaged in many conversations. "Douglas, I want to thank you for listening to me talk about mother. Because of you I think I can now say what I've been holding back since she died.

Would you mind if I told you the truth?"

"I would be honored, dear cousin."

"Well, except for that first hour I spent by Mother's beside after she passed on, I have felt such freedom. Yet, I am torn by my emotions; should I cry or be allayed—is there a need to be sad? I don't know. The truth is I feel unpardonably relieved. Do you think me dreadful?"

Captain Bradford smiled handsomely behind his trim brown mustache as he gazed at her pink lips and creamy complexion. "I do not judge you my cousin. In the past whenever Gavin and I visited you, I often felt badly for you. I could see how your mother, God rest her soul, never allowed you to think or speak for yourself. Nevertheless, I'm certain she felt all she said and did was in your best interest; perhaps her mother did the same with her. Therefore, please don't fret for my sake; I wholly understand how you feel. Doubtless, the relief is there and will be even more so when your guilt lessens. All the same, we know that your mother meant well and loved you dearly."

"She did, she did." Lillian took her handkerchief and dabbed her eyes. "I know she did, and when I see her in that light I'm honestly grieved. I think you must be right; perhaps, she simply knew no other way."

"Well so be it. I am delighted that your composure and well-being is no longer held back by her. I do so admire your determination to improve your countenance Lillian. Now if I may be bold, I confess that you look perfectly lovely tonight, just as you have ever since you arrived at Ivywood."

"Thank you Douglas. Between you and my dear brother your encouragement has been a great source of comfort to me." She looked at him warmly, with her misty blue eyes piercing deeply into his soul.

Chapter 12

After attending the Christmas Eve service at Ivywood Chapel, everyone joined together in the music room to hear the young ladies play the pianoforte and sing for everyone. "You play with such precision and delicacy, my dear sweet Audrey." James beamed with pride as he escorted her back to her seat when she had finished her performance. "Now, please don't think me too bold, but perhaps later, while everyone is busy playing cards or reading, you and I might slip away and be alone for a few minutes."

She blushed at his bold suggestion. "I love you the more for it, James. Indeed, we don't often have time together without someone following us during our walks or sitting nearby in the library." She squeezed his hand and looked up at him with her steady blue eyes, "I wish we didn't have to wait so long to be married, however, for my brother's sake and our reputation, I shall do my duty."

"Heaven knows I want us to be married sooner as well; yet duty is important too. Alas," he sighed cupping her hands in his. "We shall endure together."

"I discussed the matter with Veronica just this afternoon and bemoaned my fate to her. I told her that I wanted us to be man and wife like she and my brother. It didn't seem fair, I said, and I didn't know how I would manage such a long courtship."

James chuckled, shaking his head in mock disbelief. "You said all that my dear? Did she correct you on your forthrightness?"

"No she did not, but no sooner had I said this than I regretted complaining and asked her to forgive me. I admitted that I knew my brother would not have it otherwise."

"What had she to say for that?"

"She put her arm around me and with great encouragement reminded me that she and I could have a wonderful time planning everything. She said that we would pay particular attention to every detail of a new wardrobe from Paris, where we shall spend a month. Then she admitted that she'd spoken to my brother about our wedding being sooner. But he said there was nothing to be done for it; he would not hear of it."

James stood, his tall, slender body looming over Audrey as she sat daintily on the brocade settee. "I shall return post haste with our refreshments, at which time I wish to hear about the remainder of your conversation with you new sister."

She admired him as he walked upright towards the punch table. *He looks so smart in his brown linen jacket and dark britches, and his black boots are polished so beautifully, I can see my image in them, almost without distortion.*

He returned quickly and startled her from her reflections. "And how did you answer Lady Hunter?"

"My, I expected you to be a few more minutes, I am afraid I was daydreaming. As for my new sister and I, I told her I would happily become immersed in planning for my new wardrobe and wedding gown." Audrey sipped her cider, relishing the hot aroma and spicy taste. "And of course, because of all the other things that go with a bride's duties before her wedding, I promised not to say anything more on the matter."

"Good for you, dearest Audrey. I'm proud of you."

While everyone chatted and enjoyed their refreshment of cider, mulled wine, or coffee and tea, Phoebe Vance was to take her turn at the piano. It annoyed her greatly to see David Tristam sitting so close to Louisa Stuart as she walked past them. He, on the other hand was wholly perturbed that she went ahead of Louisa.

Louisa saw his look of consternation and asked, "Mr. Tristam, are you unwell?"

"My apologies, Miss Louisa, I am quite well. It's just that I had hoped to hear you play before now. How rude of me to be so impossible. Will you forgive me for worrying you?"

"Of course I will. Now if you can be patient a little longer, I'll ask my sister Harriet to accompany me at the pianoforte."

As Louisa waited for her turn, she thought back, remembering with great satisfaction how Veronica and Gavin had stared with looks of apprehension, as she and Harriet had approached the piano for the first time at Ivywood. *I am so thankful father insisted on a tutor to improve our talents and refine our dress and comportment. More importantly I am pleased that I am no longer fearful of performing in front of an audience.*

Louisa continued to reflect for a minute longer as she walked towards Harriet to see if she would play for her. *I am even more grateful that our tutor convinced Harriet not to attempt singing in public at all. I will never forget what the teacher said: "Instead of singing, Miss Harriet, let them praise you for your ability at the pianoforte. All you need my dear is to learn how to play the instrument with faultless grace and accomplishment. After my training you will outshine most of your peers when it comes to performing in the finest of music rooms."* Harriet was at first hurt, but once she saw peoples' reaction to her playing the pianoforte she had liked their praise and decided the tutor was right.

David's eyes followed Louisa to the piano and when she began to sing an aria from Mozart's opera Marriage of Figaro, she felt his gaze burning deep into her soul. When she finished her song, he came and stood next to her.

"Miss Louisa," he said, "would you and Miss Harriet play and sing one more piece for us?"

His handsome smile was enough for Louisa to agree to almost anything he might have asked, and his request was applauded by everyone in the room. He returned to his seat, watching and listening with great admiration. Before he realized what was happening to him, deep feelings of affection for Louisa began to wash over him; these were emotions completely unfamiliar to him. *They go beyond the fact that she possesses physical beauty with her pretty face and perfect figure*, he mused. *It is also her innocence and her curiosity that I adore.*

As her song ended, she found him standing once again by her side, where he took her arm and walked her back to their seat. "I must assure you," he leaned closer to her and spoke softly, his warm breath near her ear made her flush with excitement. "You are quite mistaken, yes quite, about your opinion of one preferring my stories to your music."

Though Edward Ramsay appeared charming to all the ladies, he consistently avoided Miss Phoebe's company. She however, was insensible to his lack of interest in her and maintained her fruitless pursuit for his attentions. Despite the fact that she was obtuse to her own situation, Mr. Tristam's attentiveness to Louisa disturbed her greatly.

"I dare say," Phoebe said, leaning toward her sister, "must your cousin hang on every word Miss Louisa utters? I am quite vexed by it. Several times now I have tried to warn him about her shortcomings, but he doesn't seem concerned at all."

"Don't fret so, sister, it's bad for your health. Moreover, there is not a thing you can do about it. My husband told me that his cousin does not care what we think, even if we are just trying to look after his best interest."

Phoebe's large, aquiline nose pointed into the air, "Well if he is too blind to see Miss Louisa's faults, then who am I to point them out, even if it is for his own good?"

"To be sure, Phoebe dear," Ursula said in all seriousness. "I fear he will not accept the benefit of your advice, and indeed, he may be the sorrier for it."

Clearly David Tristam did not care at all what his cousin's odious sisters had to say; instead he considered their conversation a reflection of their own inadequacies and character deficiencies. The more they spoke to him against Louisa, the more was his inability to resist her.

As he and Louisa sat together, she, with hands folded elegantly in her lap asked, "Would you mind telling me more about the Nile Mr. Tristam?"

"You know one does not cruise 'down' the Nile," he laughed, wanting to reach out and take her hand in his. "The water is as blue as the sky but different from the Mediterranean, which can be as tropical as it is stormy. The Nile is hot and affords little breeze and many flies, though in spite of this it is still acclaimed for its beauty. I hope to see it again one day. Am I correct in assuming, Miss Louisa that you would like to do some traveling yourself?" David asked, knowing full well the answer.

"Why yes I would, but who would not after hearing you tell about the world? Perchance someday the opportunity will arise. Alas, I have not the least idea how or when that shall come about."

"Maybe someday, Miss Louisa, you shall see the world after all. One never knows about these things." He smiled thinking, *lovely Louisa if I have anything to do with it you shall see it with me at your side.*

It was the night before the New Year's Eve Ball and everyone had retired to their rooms. While Veronica dressed for bed, Gavin walked the halls of Ivywood to ensure that all was well. It was a habit that he'd learned as a young boy from his father, and he followed it every night that he was home. When he finished his rounds, he hurried to Veronica's side and the warmth of their down quilts.

"Thank goodness for the cozy fire," he sighed putting his arm around her. "There's a bit of a chill in the air. It's started to snow again, and it's coming down quite hard."

Veronica snuggled up to him. "I am glad you've finished your walk, I thought perhaps we could visit a little. What with all the guests we have, the privacy of our rooms is the only place we can have time alone. That's not to say that I'm not enjoying everyone. I am."

"I understand what you mean dearest. Was there anything in particular you wanted to talk about?"

"Just that things seem to be turning out well for Louisa and Harriet, don't you agree?"

"It would appear so. I am happy to see our vicar is inclined to female company. He would do well to be a married man in his position. I've never seen him so jolly, though I've always enjoyed his company. I do believe also that my cousin Captain Bradford is a little taken with our cousin Lillian. She is so remarkably improved since we last saw her, I hardly recognize her. I think her time here over the past week has improved her even more."

"It's wonderful to see her in such good spirits," Veronica said following a big yawn. "As for Louisa and Mr. Tristam, I'm highly diverted."

"I am as well. I observed Miss Phoebe this evening when he asked Louisa to sing again. Miss Phoebe gave a disapproving look to that butterball of a sister, Mrs. Twackham."

Veronica burst out laughing. "Really Gavin, such a description, you are too funny." She told him about the broken chaise, as Margaret had related it to her. "She said several of the servants were laughing over the incident in the kitchen while everyone was at supper."

"Well Phoebe and her sister are a most unfortunate pair," Gavin chuckled. "One is unhappily married, and the other is destined to become the same if her desperate search for a husband succeeds."

"With her money she'll no doubt be successful; hopefully it will be with someone who deserves her." Veronica and Gavin laughed together.

"Would you like a sip of brandy?" he asked. "It might take the chill off and calm us; I think we are both a little wound up from all the company."

"I would enjoy some, thank you. There is one more thing of which I was anxious to ask your opinion." She sighed savoring the warmth of her drink. "It's certain that Miss Phoebe is making every effort to obtain some recognition from Edward Ramsay, but in my view he has little interest in her endeavors. In fact I've not seen him show one bit of partiality towards her."

"You're quite right my love. I'm gratified to see that Cousin Edward has good sense when it comes to Miss Phoebe." Gavin pulled Veronica closer to him. "I want you to know that Mrs. Anderson spoke very highly of how you seem to make each guest feel welcome, and her praise of your abilities is quite accurate. You are in my estimation the perfect mistress for Ivywood. We would be lost without you. Indeed, I don't know how I ever managed before you came into my life."

Veronica giggled. "Perhaps you just muddled through."

"Audacious madam," he laughed. "And now that you're a married woman, I will have my way with you."

He nuzzled his mouth onto her neck and tickled her sides. When she wiggled out of his grasp, she could barely catch her breath, and he saw that she suddenly looked very tired. He put his hands on her shoulders and held her away from him so he could get a better look at her.

"Are you feeling up to all the excitement these holidays have to offer? You appear a little tired, yet your cheeks have a certain glow and there's a twinkle in your eyes."

She smiled thinking, *should I tell him tonight or wait until the New Year?* "I enjoy all the fuss and family that comes with this time of year. I am quite tired though and think that I shall be asleep the minute my head hits the pillow."

"Well despite looking a little weary, you are exceptionally beautiful tonight my love." He leaned over and kissed her. "Sleep well darling."

Chapter 13

As they walked toward the ballroom, Veronica felt anxious. "Truly, Gavin, I'm a little nervous about presenting the waltz tonight at our first ball together. Are you as well?"

"Indeed not," he chuckled. "At any rate, very shortly now, it will be done and we will know soon enough if we shall be banished from country society forever." He smiled lovingly at her. "You look absolutely stunning this evening, and our guests will love you and soon get over the fact that we have introduced a little scandal into their dull lives." He patted her arm reassuringly. "Look confident now and smile and you'll be the envy of everyone here."

When they entered the ballroom, the head steward announced them; all three hundred guests held their breath at the sight of the handsome newlyweds. Veronica looked dazzling in her creamy white satin gown, which flowed gracefully down the back showing off several rows of red silk roses, each with a diamond in the center. The heart shaped neckline was trimmed in rubies and diamonds.

Gavin too presented a dashing presence in his satin, grey-striped vest set off by his black waistcoat, white britches, silk stockings and cravat. His stature and welcoming smile conveyed a vigorous and satisfied countenance as he spoke.

"Welcome to all of you," he said grandly with outstretched arms. "We are so very pleased to see everyone. Now, I must beg your indulgence and pray that this new music will not cause you to be astonished. As they do in London and Europe, I invite you to join us in our first waltz, the 'Cosa Rara'."

Gavin looked up at the orchestra and signaled for them to begin playing. The shocked crowd some filled with awe and others showing their disapproval could not keep their eyes off Veronica and Gavin. Those with admiration for the couple thought it astounding that the bride and groom had the power to begin their first ball with a dance that many had never seen, but had only heard described as scandalous. Albeit, no one could help but have a high regard for the newlyweds—they were stunning. They seemed to glide without effort into the middle of the ballroom, as though on a cloud. They twirled and waltzed around the room as if they had been doing so all their lives.

"Look Gavin," Veronica whispered. "Everyone is staring. I certainly hope someone will join us." She looked up with a gleam in her eyes and a beaming smile. "Yet, I must confess that despite what our guests might think, I adore this music and the dance. Might I add dearest, you're quite the handsomest fellow in the room. Indeed, I am certain that I'm the envy of the entire company of ladies present."

"Thank you, I'm sorry but you are wrong. The one to be envied is me, for your beauty surpasses all." He brushed his lips through her soft dark curls and whispered, "Now don't you worry about our guests, someone will follow and then others will too."

Over the resounding majesty of the music and the radiance of the newlyweds, murmurs of disapproval mixed with outright veneration, echoed throughout the room. The beauty of the striking lovers continued to intoxicate the crowd as they watched in wonder. After several minutes, the first to join the Hunters in the waltz was David Tristam with his strong arms gracefully guiding Louisa Stuart.

Louisa felt as though she were pirouetting in a dream, where one dances on air and the exhilaration is greater than anything. But in her dreams she had never had a partner as elegant and exciting as Mr. Tristam; she hoped the dream would never end.

Nor could David in his wildest fantasy conceive that such sweetness existed for him, until he experienced the joy of holding in his arms Miss Louisa Stuart. *She has stolen my heart, and I want to drift around the room with her forever in her liveliness, charm and innocence, which teases me insensibly.*

"Miss Louisa, dare I ask?" he inquired with deference and a pounding heart. "Have you waltzed before? Clearly, you are more than able to follow my lead as though you have."

"I am all astonishment that I enjoy the sway of this music, having never heard it. However, I have always taken great pleasure in dancing, and I am most at ease following you." Her cheeks glowed because of his closeness. "May I ask? Where did you learn to waltz? It's obvious you have done so before. Indeed, it is all very exhilarating."

"The waltz is, of course, well received in Paris and many other parts of Europe. Certainly, I prefer it to the parlor dancing we've done while waiting impatiently for this ball. I'm pleased the Hunters have chosen to allow it."

David looked into Louisa's large blue eyes and smiled. *She's so fresh and agile in my arms.* "If you'd not consider me insolent, Miss Louisa, may I speak boldly and say that grace and beauty run in your family?"

"Mr. Tristam, you are bold," Louisa said, unable once again to keep the color from her cheeks.

Unused to the company of young ladies who still blushed, her lack of guile captivated him. "It is the truth," he replied almost in a whisper.

Some time after the excitement of the waltz had passed, the ball went forward and everyone seemed to be having a good time. In particular, the Vicar John Boswell and Harriet Stuart had become engrossed in conversation, as was their usual way of enjoying each other's company. However, tonight they were especially pleased to

97

express their opinions about her sister's introduction of the waltz.

"Imagine the audacity," Harriet said, "to allow such a scandalous display of decadence. Watching my sister and her husband hold each other close for such a period of time as the dance recommends, combined with their rapid turning movements, it is no wonder that the waltz is thought to be indecent and reckless."

"Indeed, Miss Harriet, I agree. People talk about the dance in London as if it were no different than the allemande. And, I understand that famous dance masters see it as a threat to their profession. The waltz is easily learned, where as the allemande or the minuet and other court dances require knowing complex figures, along with suitable posture and deportment."

"You're quite right sir. Nonetheless, I'm certain there are some here who thought it was highly amusing and enjoyed every minute of the dissipated display."

"I'm sure you are correct in your observation, and I am very glad we, you and I that is, are of the same opinion. However, now a more proper set is about to begin." Boswell cleared his throat nervously. "Would you allow me the honor?"

"I'd be delighted."

"Yes, it is high time we took our turn on the dance floor. And may I say Miss Harriet that you dance beautifully. I think we should do this a little more often."

"Thank you Mr. Boswell, but you are too kind. Dare I say that I enjoy dancing with you as well sir?"

"I'm pleased to hear it." After a few moments of thought, Boswell cleared his throat and began to feel the heat rise to his face. "Miss Harriet, I have something very particular I would like to ask you."

"Mr. Boswell, are you well?"

"Of course," he stammered. "But perhaps we should sit down."

He took her elbow and led her to a settee that offered a bit of privacy. "Oh Miss Harriet," he began, "would I be too daring after such a brief time to tell you how much I admire and love you? No," he paused and wiped his brow. "I must be bold. After all, someone with your qualities ought not to be overlooked. Will you marry me dearest

Harriet, please? I've waited all my life for someone like you, and I thought for certain I would never be so fortunate." He reached for her hands, his face still flush. "Almost from the moment we met, I felt you were the perfect partner for me. Then after spending these past weeks together, I knew with all my heart that I wanted you for my wife."

All at once she realized that despite his strong, steady presence, she needed to take charge of the situation. "Mr. Boswell, oh John, yes; my answer is yes. However, might I suggest that to prevent foolish talk about us just having met, that we keep our engagement a secret for at least a fortnight?"

"Harriet, Harriet, you have made me very happy. You are so wise. It is an excellent idea! Of course, why didn't I think of it? We'll tell no one until then. Oh dearest, tell me true. Do you love me as I love you?"

"Yes John, I do love you; though I have not wanted to admit it to myself for fear of being disappointed. Now that you have professed your love for me, I am happier than I ever thought possible."

"Beautiful Harriet, your love will always be requited." He beamed with elation, still holding tightly to her hands.

Harriet sat for a moment, and then she let out a heavy sigh wondering, *where did my words come from? Never mind that, one thing is for certain, I would be quite foolish to play coy and pretend that I don't care for him. After all it is the only proposal I have received, and I do love him.*

"Oh John, we shall be so happy together," she said staring at his high forehead, straight nose and strong chin. "I never thought someone as handsome and wonderful as you would now become a part of my life." She smiled at him and dabbed her handkerchief to her eyes.

"You are my true love," he sighed reaching up to touch her cheek. "I promise I shall cherish you forever."

Phoebe Vance could not have been more thrilled when Edward Ramsay took a seat next to her. However, for his part it was merely a convenient place to sit, and he did not consider himself having any particular good fortune to be there. *Alas, he mused, her conversation does not interest me, but I will be polite. If only she didn't have such a fearsome nose equal only to her disposition, I might not be quite so distracted. Yet there is something intriguing about that appendage. I wonder if it is that which makes her homely, or is she homely despite its size and shape?*

Misguided by his intense study of her and the fact that he chose to sit by her, Phoebe was inspired to begin conversation. "Tell me Mr. Ramsay, what is it like in America?"

He took a minute before responding, as he realized that he had been staring. "Americans are a stubborn lot, but extremely industrious. Cotton and tobacco are king in South Carolina, and it is a mighty beautiful country. Nonetheless, they favor slavery in the southern states, and I am against it."

"Was it a grand property you owned, and do you miss your home?" she asked."

"It is still grand Miss Phoebe," he said, looking for an excuse to move on. "I miss some things about it. We have about a hundred and fifty square miles of land, some of which the tenants and factory workers farm for their own needs." He looked around hoping to escape, but then the music began. "Ah yes, a waltz, would you do me the honor of this dance?" He reached out his hand deciding it would be rude to leave. "I must say, I am gratified that my cousin has seen fit to entertain us with such delightful music. I trust Miss Phoebe that you waltz, coming from London and all?"

"Indeed, most London society, either in court or at private parties, know how," Phoebe answered, elated for his asking. "I have to admit I am amazed that Mr. Hunter has brought the waltz to the countryside. Certainly, I'm even more surprised that his wife allowed him to do so."

"What, pray tell, does his wife have to do with it?"

"Well," she answered insensible to his scorn, "she is from the country you know. Country society in England is a bit restricted. This is especially true when it comes to the more advanced and sophisticated things in this world."

"Really, do tell!" he said. "I find the warmth, charm and beauty of Lady Hunter far less confining than the mockery of the self-proclaimed elite from London." At that moment the music ended and without another word Edward returned Phoebe to their previous location, bowed and turned away.

Before the orchestra performed its huge drum roll announcing the New Year, Gavin thanked everyone for coming, and then made the announcement of Audrey's engagement. This was followed by the sweet resonance of Auld Lang Syne.

"Well, my love," Gavin said to Veronica, "I'm eager to taste your first of many New Year kisses."

"And I as well," she sighed, suddenly feeling very warm. "Gavin, I—"

"Veronica!" he shouted, as she fainted in his arms.

He carried her across the hall into the library and laid her down on one of the divans. Just then her father came in with his wife in tow; James and Audrey followed with Colette and Basil.

"Quick," Gavin ordered a nearby servant, "fetch the doctor." Then he asked Audrey, "Can you have Douglas come in for me dear sister?"

As Audrey turned to leave, Gavin saw that Veronica had opened her eyes. "Oh darling, what is the matter?" he asked.

She put her hand to his cheek and whispered, "I only fainted. Why don't you ask everyone to return to the ball? I will be fine."

When Douglas came in, he saw Gavin wiping Veronica's brow with his kerchief. "Is she all right?" he asked, fearing the worst. "Tell me what I can do."

"She seems to be well enough, considering. Just the same, we have sent for the doctor," Gavin said. "If you would see to our guests and take over for me, I would be much obliged."

"Certainly, I'll take care of everything. Don't worry about the guests. If you need me further, just send a servant for me."

"Don't look so worried darling," Veronica smiled when they were alone. "I had planned to tell you tonight when we went to bed, but I'll tell you now. I believe we are going to have a child. I have thought so for several weeks."

Ecstatic with joy and relief, he kissed her hand and cheek. "Dearest, loveliest Veronica, this is absolutely the most excellent news. I could not be more pleased."

Mr. and Mrs. Stuart were thrilled to hear of another grandchild on the way. However, two weeks later this news was nearly out done by Harriet's announcement that she and John Boswell were to be married in June. He, of course, had asked her father for her hand and, holding back a sigh of relief, Mr. Stuart had willingly granted his permission with blessings.

Mrs. Stuart was so ecstatic over this betrothal that she all but fainted at hearing the news. "To think that my most troublesome daughter is to be married in six months," she expounded. "The excitement is almost too much to bear, but bear it I shall and with great pleasure. Imagine, she'll be the wife of a clergyman; how fitting, how perfect."

"And Mother," Harriet said, "We will have a living that may not be lavish, but between his five hundred a year and mine we shall live quite nicely by my standards."

"Oh yes," Louisa said. "And your parish home is already charming, with very pleasant appointments and a lovely park as well."

"To be sure," Veronica said. "In addition Gavin and I plan to do a little refurbishing and make some improvements before you and Mr. Boswell are married."

"That's most generous of you sister," Harriet smiled.

"Well now that you're spoken for Harriet," Mrs. Stuart interrupted, "all that's needed is for Louisa to make an attachment with Mr. Tristam."

"Mother, please!" Louisa exclaimed, her face turning bright red. "There is nothing between Mr. Tristam and myself. Didn't he leave just two days ago with nothing more than a simple good-bye?"

"That may be, my dear," replied her mother, "but you mark my words, he favors you. I know these things. I see him when he looks at you, though he thinks no one is watching. He paid you very particular attention during his stay here, and there is no doubt in my mind that something will come of it."

"Oh mother, how can you think such a thing? After all, a man of his distinction, with wealth and charm, can have any woman he chooses, preferably someone with great riches and connections. I have neither; therefore I refuse to put my hope where it should not be."

She sighed thinking sadly how she would miss his remarkable, soul piercing eyes, one of the many things which compelled her to be drawn to him. "No indeed that would be very foolish of me."

Chapter 14

It was March, and the weather was cold with some scattered snow on the ground and in the hills. "The ride to Glenvalley has been very enjoyable," Veronica said to Gavin as they approached Basil and Colette's estate.

Gavin smiled, adjusting his leather gloves. "We've certainly been blessed with perfect weather, and fortunately between here and Ivywood the roads were clear."

"Oh look, darling," Veronica pointed. "I can see Glenvalley from here. It will only be a few more minutes now."

When the Hunters arrived, Basil and Colette met them as they stepped out of the carriage. "Welcome, my dear sister and brother," Basil said greeting them with outstretched arms. "I hope your trip was pleasant and that you are well? We're so glad you've come for the birth of our first child next month. You do us a great honor by agreeing to be the baby's Godparents."

"We were pleased to be asked." Gavin patted his friend on the back. "It's good to be here."

Veronica gave her sister a hug. "It's wonderful to see you both again."

"I'm glad you've arrived safely," Collette said, giving Veronica a kiss on the cheek.

"It is an easy four hour ride," Gavin remarked taking Veronica's arm.

Basil pulled his pocket watch out. "It's nearly one o'clock. We will have some cake and tea after you refresh yourselves, and then supper will be served around four."

"I for one," Veronica chuckled, "or should I say three, am quite hungry."

"Pray tell, what are you laughing about sister?" Basil queried with an amused smile.

"Perhaps I should not speak of such a thing," she replied. "But I don't think I can keep it from you a moment longer."

"What is it?" Colette looked at her quizzically.

"Do you mind Gavin if I tell them now?"

"I think we had better get out of the cold first," he answered. "I wouldn't want the three of you to catch a chill."

Colette started to giggle and the moment they entered the Vance's generous foyer, she said, "I have guessed your secret dear sister. You're going to have twins. When did you find out and why didn't you write me about it?"

"The doctor told us a month ago, but I wanted to surprise you."

Basil grinned and patted Gavin's shoulder. "Allow me to congratulate you my friend. You must be delighted."

"We were taken aback, but of course, pleased indeed." Gavin grinned, "And now twins aside, my friend, I'm putting you on your guard. In my good humor I will have no mercy on you at billiards, and I am quite ready to abuse you at whist." He looked kindly at Colette. "Forgive me dear sister. I should have more consideration for your condition, but I could not possibly allow that husband of yours any advantage."

"I hope Colette," Veronica smiled, "that my husband will be kind to you, that is if you are up for some cards."

"I do seem to tire easily," Colette replied moving her hand over her stomach. "Nevertheless, I am certain you can count on me for awhile."

Later that evening after supper and cards, Gavin and Basil withdrew to the billiard room, while Veronica and Colette retired to the Hunter guest suite. "It is wonderful to have you and Gavin here, and learning that you're having twins is most happy news. Mother and Father will be thrilled. By the way, Mother is eager for both of you to dine with them tomorrow. Basil and I have declined the invitation, for we visit Hedgerow at least once a week. At any rate, I'll be happy to take my afternoon nap while you're gone."

"I am sure you will be missed. You look well dear; I hope you are feeling the same. It's too soon for me to notice any changes yet, but before long I will be looking like you. Now Colette I must remark how excellent everything looks at Glenvalley. It was very agreeable before you put your hand to it, but clearly you have made it quite elegant. How do you find it?"

"Glenvalley definitely needed a woman's touch, and I have enjoyed redecorating some of the rooms. Basil gives me a free hand with whatever I want to do, and sometimes rather than he and I shopping for things, I ask mother to attend me. She has quite the time of it. I believe she finds a great deal of enjoyment in helping me spend Basil's money." Colette sighed and looked around the room. "Do you think Veronica that we could ever have imagined the freedom wealth affords?"

"I marvel frequently when I see how differently our lives have turned out from what we might have expected. After all, true love and riches rarely go hand in hand. We are very fortunate indeed." Veronica stretched and yawned. "Oh Colette all of a sudden I feel very sleepy. I believe the day's journey has caught up with me."

"Before I retire for the evening," Colette said, "I wanted to see your new gown for our Glenvalley Ball."

Veronica asked Margaret to bring down her pink satin gown from Paris. "Fortunately I can still be out in my condition. But what about you dearest, it is hardly fitting for you to be among the guests two weeks before the baby is due."

"This is true, and I told Basil I was most unhappy to be hidden away. He comforted me by saying that this being the country he thinks I might not be chastised for slipping quietly down stairs to sit with you. You and I can enjoy watching everyone and visit at the same time."

"Well that will be nice for us. Now tell me about the Gerard dinner party next week."

"Next week is Sarah's seventeenth birthday, and her mother and father want to celebrate it with dinner and dancing at their estate."

"Do I understand correctly that for the party and the ball, Miss Phoebe and the Twackhams, as well as the Ramsays and Captain Bradford are coming?"

Colette yawned, "Yes, and they will all be staying here. Lillian wrote and asked if we minded that the Captain come along. Of course, we're delighted; there is plenty of room. And in Miss Phoebe's letter she said that David Tristam is planning to be here too."

"Does Louisa know?"

"No," Colette laughed good-naturedly. "I thought I'd let that be a surprise. Since she's so inclined to think there is nothing between them, we will see what happens."

"You're absolutely right. There's no sense in stirring up her hopes, even if she says she has none with regards to him." Veronica moved over to her dressing table and began to let down her hair. "Imagine if Louisa were to form an attachment with someone of David Tristam's stature. She'd be the talk of the town, in fact the whole of London society."

"Truly that is so, and Mother might die from the excitement of it." Colette grinned, putting her hands on her stomach as the baby kicked inside. "Speaking of engagements, I think Captain Bradford has a fondness for Lillian Ramsay, but Basil says it is too soon since her mother's death for her to consider him. Do you think there could be anything between them?"

"Gavin believed that at Twelfth Night an attachment was

beginning to form, but I can't say. Certainly it would be a nice thing for both of them, though it may be too much for her to consider at this time." Veronica yawned, "I'm quite ready for sleep my dear, I think I will ask Margaret to help me prepare for bed now."

"You're right, it is time." Colette stood to hug Veronica good night. "Indeed, it will be very exciting at Glenvalley with everyone here."

The next day after a leisurely morning with Colette and Basil, Veronica and Gavin took the fifteen minute ride to see her parents at Hedgerow. When they arrived Mr. Stuart greeted them, bowing to Gavin and giving his daughter a kiss on the cheek. "Veronica, Mr. Hunter, how well you both look."

"We are so pleased to see you." Mrs. Stuart offered, still aflame at the idea of her daughter's new wealth. "We hope your trip yesterday was pleasant. Please sit down. Mr. Stuart is entirely correct, you look very well indeed."

"Thank you, we had an excellent ride yesterday," Gavin replied, amused by their informality, yet he admired their pleasant, unpretentious home.

"It's wonderful to see you," Veronica said excitedly. "But I cannot keep silent any longer without telling you our news."

"Tell us what?" Mrs. Stuart queried anxiously.

Gavin laughed. "I think your mother may swoon if she is forced to wait another moment."

At hearing about twins Mrs. Stuart fanned herself excitedly. "Oh my, this is the best news I have heard in a Bastille. To think I will have three grandchildren now before the year is out. I'm sure your father is overjoyed. As for me, I believe the anticipation is almost more than I am able to bear."

"We are indeed delighted for you both," Mr. Stuart said. "Nonetheless, despite my elation over the news of more grandchildren, I hope, Lord Hunter, that you will do me the honor of accompanying me to my library? I dare say, there we may find some quiet from the chatter of these happy women. Let us leave them to their discourses over matters that concern them."

"Certainly," Gavin bowed as they took their leave.

He was used to the Stuarts, especially since the holidays. He enjoyed Mr. Stuart's company; Mrs. Stuart he tolerated with amusement. He wondered how Veronica could have descended from such as her mother. Gavin believed that in their youth Mr. and Mrs. Stuart had perhaps been a handsome couple. But now in Mrs. Stuart he saw a lost beauty, which came with age and in her case much self indulgence. Mr. Stuart, however, had integrity in business, if not in raising his daughters and controlling his wife. He carried an air of dignity about him and looked quite distinguished with touches of silver-gray hair.

"Veronica," her mother said tucking the lace at the bodice of her green gown, "You are looking very good, and how is Colette?"

"She is fine. She asked me to extend you and father, and my sisters, an invitation to join her and Mr. Vance for supper tomorrow. She wanted me to remind you that it will be nothing quite so formal as the Gerard's dinner party next week."

Veronica studied Louisa for a minute and saw maturity where she once lacked, and innocent beauty that had blossomed. "Louisa you look wonderful. May I assume that you and Mr. Tristam have corresponded with each other since the holidays?"

"We have not," Louisa said, feeling color come to her cheeks. "I am astonished you would think so. Indeed, what would we write to each other about?" She put her hands to her face and smiled. "However, just yesterday I received a post from him, much to my surprise. He said he would arrive, not only for the ball at Glenvalley, but for the Gerard party. He hoped I would not be too busy to invite him for tea. Well of course, I'd never pass him off so foolishly, though it's hardly believable that he would want to form an attachment with anyone such as myself, who has so little to offer."

"You should not talk that way. Don't forget my dear sister," Veronica said sternly, "we are the daughters of a gentleman and that makes us equal with all gentlemen's children, regardless of how little our fortunes and connections are. In addition Louisa, you can't overlook the fact that Mr. Tristam wanted to let you know he is coming. No doubt this is some indication of his affection for you."

Louisa stepped over to look out the parlor window. "Veronica, you have much confidence."

Veronica sighed, wishing Louisa was more self-assured, and then she turned to Harriet and said, "I dare say the prospect of marriage has brightened your countenance. I brought a letter from your Vicar and also a message that he asked me to deliver. He wanted you to know he will arrive in time for the ball."

"Thank you Veronica." Harriet reached for Mr. Boswell's letter. "If you don't mind, I'd like to read this in private."

When Harriet left the room, Veronica handed her mother a small purse. "Here is a little something from Mr. Hunter and me."

When Mrs. Stuart looked in the purse, she burst our in tears, "My dear child, how very kind of you."

"What is it?" Louisa asked, trying to peer over her mother's shoulder.

"It's five one hundred pound bank notes to help prepare Harriet for her wedding clothes and gown. I think now, each of us shall also be able to have new gowns for the Gerard's dinner party and for the ball. Indeed, I believe we can replenish our entire wardrobes with this much. How kind of you my dear daughter," Mrs. Stuart said giving Veronica a big hug. "Thank you, you have made me very happy, and I'm sure your father will be pleased too. Now he won't have anything to complain about regarding money for his youngest daughter's marriage."

"Louisa run and fetch your sister," Mrs. Stuart ordered. "I want to share this good news with her. I think she was a bit concerned as to how we would manage."

As soon as Louisa and Harriet came down, it was clear that Louisa had informed her of what Veronica had done. Harriet ran over to her and gave her a big hug. "Thank you dear, dear sister, thank you."

Mrs. Stuart went on and on, catching her breath in between thoughts. "Oh my girls, I am so proud of you. I just can't help myself for boasting over how agreeably you have each fared. I dare say

Louisa, all we have to do now is get you settled and the matter will be finished. Imagine the Stuart girls' married to such wealth; I always knew it would be so."

"How is Gabriella?" Veronica interrupted. "I have not heard from her in a long while, except to say they could not come for Twelfth Night."

"Why, she is just fine and her letters, few and infrequent as they are, say how eager she is to return to Hedgerow to see everyone. They should be arriving in about a fortnight, just in time for the Glenvalley Ball. She seemed quite delighted that Harriet is getting married. And she is especially eager to hear all about Louisa's prospects with Mr. Tristam."

Before returning to Colette and Basil's, the Hunters dined at Hedgerow where Mrs. Stuart put on an impressive feast of roasted duck and berry pie. During supper, she thanked Gavin and Veronica for their generous gift and assured them that the very first day of good weather they would set off for a shopping trip to London.

"Wife," Mr. Stuart said cheerfully, jumping at the opportunity to have his home to himself. "Why don't you and your unmarried daughters go to London tomorrow and spend a few days? There is plenty of time to return with a day or two to spare before the Gerard's dinner party."

"Oh, my dear Mr. Stuart, how will you manage without us?" Mrs. Stuart asked.

"Let me assure you," he paused and chuckled. "I will do very well in your absence just knowing that you're having a wonderful time spending money that you came by so freely. Tomorrow I will take the chaise over to Colette's for supper. Please don't concern yourself about me."

"Father's right, Mother," Louisa declared. "Let's go. I long for a new ball gown."

By nine o'clock the next morning Louisa, Harriet and their mother had begun their four hour carriage ride to London, eager to spend their new found wealth.

Chapter 15

After five days in London, Mrs. Stuart, Louisa and Harriet arrived home around three in the afternoon. By three-thirty they had their packages open and spread all over the parlor to show off to their father. In the midst of the excitement, a servant came in and announced that Louisa had a visitor.

"It's Mr. David Tristam. Shall I show him in?"

Louisa's heart jumped into her throat, as she quickly tried to make the parlor presentable. "Mother, what shall we do? Can you and Harriet make haste and help me take this into Father's study?"

"Not on your life," Mr. Stuart laughed. "You'll not bring this disarray anywhere near my study. You'll have to find some place else. But never mind, Louisa. I'll step into the hall and greet Mr. Tristam for you."

Finally when the servants had carried everything upstairs, Mrs. Stuart motioned for Mr. Tristam to be shown into the parlor. Seeing David standing in the doorway, Louisa suddenly felt an indescribable joy mixed with wonder—*he is actually calling on us in our humble abode.*

He bowed calmly to Mrs. Stuart, then Harriet and lastly to Louisa. "It is a pleasure to see you again. I hope I'm not interrupting anything?"

"Not at all," Mrs. Stuart said. "You're very welcome indeed. Won't you have some tea? Moreover, why don't you stay for supper? There is plenty; this morning I instructed cook to prepare a large pork roast."

David looked at Louisa, and her smile convinced him that he should accept. "Well if you insist, it would be my pleasure."

"Yes Mr. Tristam, I'm sure Father would welcome your company." Harriet tittered, "He always says there are far too many women in the house for his liking."

"When did you arrive in town Mr. Tristam?" Louisa inquired nervously.

"I just rode in from London and as I had to pass by here on the way to Glenvalley, I thought it proper to stop and pay my respects. I understand you returned from London yourselves only an hour ago. Did you have a pleasant trip?"

"It was wonderful," Mrs. Stuart answered. "Perhaps you did not know, but my youngest here, Harriet, is to be married in June. We were shopping for her wedding clothes and had a grand time." She smiled at Louisa then said, "We'll be serving supper at seven o'clock. In the meantime I'm sure Mr. Tristam would like to see our park. Louisa, it is such a beautiful day why don't you show him."

Louisa turned bright red and looked at Harriet, "Would you like to join us?"

After their cup of tea Harriet and Louisa put on their coats, and the three of them walked outside together. Just as they entered the garden, Harriet asked Louisa if she minded her leaving them to pay a visit to their neighbor Sarah Gerard.

Louisa smiled timidly. "I think Mr. Tristam and I can manage the park alone."

"Absolutely, Miss Harriet," David agreed. "You must not let us keep you from enjoying your friend."

"I'll meet you back at the house for supper." Harriet waved as she ran towards Sarah's place, which was about a quarter of a mile down the road.

"Miss Louisa," David said looking around, "you have lovely grounds. It's really quite pleasant here. Thank you for walking with me."

"Well, our park is small, and I am sure you have seen much grander properties."

"It's true, I have. But I can attest to the fact that I've not had the pleasure of seeing one with such a charming guide by my side." He smiled handsomely at her and knew that his compliment bordered on being impertinent. "Forgive me for being bold, Miss Louisa."

She made no reply. However, she felt certain that the color in her cheeks most assuredly matched the red roses in their garden. She could barely endure the excitement she felt walking with him.

"Miss Louisa," he said as he stopped and smelled one of the roses, "may I pick one for my lapel, one to remember our walk by?"

"Of course, please do."

"Actually, why don't you choose one for me, and I'll cut it with my pocket knife."

She decided upon a beautiful yellow rose and shyly pointed to it. "I think that one is perfect."

While putting the rose in his jacket's buttonhole, he wondered what her parents would think. But he said nothing and instead asked, "Miss Louisa, may I stop by tomorrow and perhaps we could take a leisurely stroll into town? I was hoping that you and your sister might show me the best shops, as I have never been into your little burg of Broomfield."

"That would be quite enjoyable. I know I don't have any plans, but for my sister I cannot speak. We shall ask her at supper. And she is right about you staying to dine with us. Father will be pleased to have another gentleman at our table."

"I'm looking forward to this evening. Now for tomorrow, does one o'clock suit you?" He smelled his flower and smiled at her.

"That is a good time, yes." She felt jittery and excited at the same time as they walked back to the house. *Could he truly care for me,* she wondered?

At the celebration party in honor of Sarah Gerard's seventeenth birthday it was easy to see why her parents had not allowed her out sooner. Gracefully tall and charming, her deep blue eyes and creamy complexion contrasted with her long black curls. Because of her beauty she was sought after by nearly every eligible bachelor present, young and old. This was most particularly true of Edward Ramsay.

After an extraordinary banquet of sumptuous delights, Colette and Veronica sat together and watched the parlor dancing for which the Gerard's had hired a trio to play music.

"Poor Miss Phoebe," Colette whispered to Veronica. "It would seem that Mr. Ramsay is quite taken with our pretty neighbor tonight. I am happy to see Sarah finally out. She has done little else these last couple of years except whine to me how much she wished she had the same freedom you and I had before we were seventeen. During the holidays with you, I thought I could not bear another word about the matter from her."

"Honestly, my dear Colette, it's time for her to be out, and I must say, I have never seen her look so lovely." Veronica spoke in a whisper and nodded towards Lillian Ramsay. "Have you noticed how wonderful she looks?"

"I think that Captain Bradford might agree with you," Colette chuckled. "I've not seen him leave her side all evening."

Lillian Ramsay would not have believed that her life could be so changed since her long-lost half-brother had moved into Lochaven with her. She had insisted that he do so.

"You must come and live with Miss Rosemary and me," she maintained. "After all, Edward, you have no relatives here in England, and Lochaven is far too large for just my companion and me."

"You're quite right about family," he agreed. "Since I don't have plans to return to America, other than to pay an occasional visit to my business in South Carolina, I think moving to Lochaven is a capital idea."

Along with the joy of having Edward living with her, Lillian had been quite gratified by the correspondence between herself and Douglas Bradford. His letters were frequent and contained many inquiries as to her health and that of Edward's. The Captain had also declared how much he looked forward to seeing her again.

"*Most regrettably,*" his last letter had said, "*I am very sorry that I have not had the opportunity to come to Lochaven sooner. Regimental duties have occupied more of my time than I wanted, especially when I would rather have been visiting with you.*"

When Douglas arrived at the Ramsay's to ride with Lillian and Edward to Glenvalley, she had to admit to herself that her feelings for Douglas were more than friendship.

"Lillian, I've missed our conversations since Twelfth Night at Ivywood." Douglas spoke freely, his sincere brown eyes gazing intently into hers as they danced at the Gerard's party. "I was pleased to read in your letters how well you are doing."

"I am, indeed, though I do sometimes miss Mother's way. After all she was very domineering and left me with little knowledge of how to do many things. God rest her soul, she would not be pleased if she knew that I fired the old housekeeper and have become very fond of Edward's, who came with him. She has taught me what my mother would have considered beneath my station. Nevertheless, I enjoy discussing with her the menus and how the household should be run. She is very kind and always willing to teach me."

"That's wonderful Lillian. I must say something agrees with you, for if you'll allow me to be bold, you look very well." He smiled, feeling an affection toward her that went beyond what he could express.

It pleased David Tristam to have spent the past two days with Louisa. He liked her family, though he was not used to her mother's zeal, which he counted as enthusiasm for life in general; she was a refreshing change for him. When he was with the Stuarts it was such a contrast to his family. The Tristam's day to day living was worse than dull; generally if anyone spoke in more than a whisper they were considered unseemly, and if you laughed too loud it was positively shocking. David found Mr. Stuart to be quite sophisticated for a country attorney. Mr. Stuart and he had discussed politics, business, Christianity and country living; David was surprised to learn that they agreed on most issues.

"You see Mr. Tristam," Mr. Stuart had said, "I desired to raise my family here in the country so that my daughters would not be subjected to the decadence of a large city such as London. The trade off notwithstanding, is that I knew my girls would have to be content with a living that was less than others of their station. Albeit, five hundred a year each for the three youngest is nothing to laugh at."

"No indeed sir, it is not," David granted. "I must commend you on the fine job you have done in bringing up your daughters. I cannot find fault with any one of them."

As David and Louisa parlor danced at the Gerard party, he said, "I see Miss Louisa that your voice is as beautiful and captivating as it was during the holidays." He smiled, admiring the bodice of her yellow satin gown. "It was good to hear you sing again tonight."

"Thank you, Mr. Tristam. You know there was a time when I would have rather died than sing in front of strangers."

"I certainly hope that you don't consider me a stranger." He looked disappointed, "I should feel very hurt if that were the case."

"Oh no," her eyes saddened. "I did not mean that at all. Indeed, I'm quite honored to hear that you are fond of my singing. Please forgive me if I gave the wrong impression. I would not hurt your feelings for the world, but I fear I might have."

"I see that you are in earnest, and I believe you. Don't fret, I do not feel slighted." He smiled as he walked her to her seat. "I hope Miss Louisa that we shall have many more dances this evening. I'll return after I have given the other gentlemen here an opportunity to dance with you. I would not want to be considered rude by keeping you all to myself."

She watched him go thinking *if only he knew that I wished him never to leave my side.*

The next day after the Gerard party, Colette and Veronica sat in the morning room while Gavin and Basil went out with the other men to shoot game. It was Basil's favorite sport and the primary reason he liked living in the country. Veronica and Colette were happy for an opportunity to visit and discuss events from the night before.

"Now tell me," Colette said, "what did you think of the party last evening? I believe Mr. Tristam is showing a very particular regard for Louisa."

"There is no doubt in my mind," Veronica laughed. "Proof of his fondness for her was not only at the Gerard's, but she says he came to Hedgerow two days together to take tea. She said that he also asked her to walk with him into Broomfield again."

"Despite all this, Louisa still goes on about feeling unworthy of his attentions." Colette sighed, "Regardless of what she says, I know she likes him very much, perhaps she is even in love with him."

"I agree." Veronica chuckled, "But Miss Phoebe is not pleased. I overheard her whisper a reprehensible remark to her sister while they watched Mr. Tristam dance with Louisa two sets one right after the other. Miss Phoebe asked Mrs. Twackham what she thought her husband's cousin could possibly see in someone of such little significance."

"How arrogant," Colette said. "Miss Phoebe is most irritating. I had no idea she would say such a thing in your hearing. To think I was beginning to feel sorry for her last night because of Mr. Ramsay's attentions to Sarah. I'll not make that mistake again."

"It's clear to me that Miss Phoebe doesn't deserve your sympathy, and her resentment towards all of us is uncalled for. I am gratified that Edward recognizes her lack of character; he deserves credit for his insight."

"Yes," Colette grinned. "I'm thrilled that Miss Phoebe and her sister went to London for a couple of days, though we shall have to suffer their company for awhile longer when they return. I understand they are heading for Brighton right after the ball, but they will return after the baby is born. For Basil's sake I will endure their presence."

"I'll be here to suffer with you my dear. Perhaps we can encourage them to take a few more trips into town," Veronica laughed. "Now on a serious note Colette, Gavin and I want you and Basil to attend us at the birth of the twins. We'd be honored if you would consent to be their Godparents."

"Oh Veronica, yes, I am sure I can speak for both of us. We would be delighted. It will be wonderful to share that time with you."

"Thank you, I know it will please Gavin to hear that you've accepted. He said you would."

Chapter 16

Anticipation for the Glenvalley Ball created excitement for everyone planning to attend, including the regiment that was in town. Basil had promised to host a spring ball when he and Colette returned from their honeymoon. At that time neither had given a thought to the fact that she might be heavy with child.

"I shall have to be content with observation," Colette said to Veronica as they sat and watched the ball progress. "At least you can still dance."

"I am enjoying myself sitting here with you. To watch the nuances of those seeking a partner for life is quite amusing." Veronica laughed quietly, covering her mouth with her hand. "Just look at Sarah Gerard. She looks lovelier than ever this evening, and I thought that at her birthday party she could not have been more beautiful."

"She is quite stunning," Colette agreed. "It is understandable that the gentlemen seek her favor."

"Indeed, and she treats each one she dances with as if he were the only person in the room. Edward Ramsay does the same with his partners, but tonight it is apparent he favors her above all others."

Colette smiled wryly. "I have noticed, and I've been watching Miss Phoebe. She does not appear to be pleased with the way things are going."

Indeed, Phoebe Vance was feeling quite sorry for herself as she watched Edward dance a second set with Sarah Gerard. *I wonder if Mr. Ramsay will ever take notice of me*, she questioned. *Since he arrived at Glenvalley, he has hardly spoken more than a civil good morning.*

This evening she had taken an extra hour at her dressing table in hopes of attracting his attention. How she hated her straw-like hair and the fuss it took to keep it in place; no matter how much she shrieked at her maid, her hideous hair seemed impossible to curl. Somehow though, the maid had managed it for this evening. When Phoebe left her room, she felt pretty in her expensive blue silk gown, which did its best to flatter her shapeless figure.

"I think sister," Phoebe said to Ursula when they entered the ballroom together, "I might be able to capture Mr. Ramsay's eye this evening."

An hour later when he had not so much as acknowledged her presence, she realized that her efforts had been for naught. With great disappointment, she decided to indulge herself at the buffet table. She became deep in thought, choosing which delicacies to select, and did not notice the tall gentlemen in uniform walking towards her with Mr. Gerard.

Though Mr. Gerard was a prominent country gentleman of means, Phoebe considered him little more than a bumpkin; she preferred the city and its society. She had been glad when she moved in with Ursula and her husband in London. She had not realized how much she missed the city until her brother had asked her to leave. *In the long run, inasmuch as it hurt me*, she mused, *Basil did me a favor by sending me away.*

"Miss Phoebe," Mr. Gerard said, intruding on her solitude, "may I present a dear friend of mine, Admiral Weatherby."

Thomas Weatherby of the Royal Navy had been in Her Majesty's Service for over twenty years and had just returned from being at sea for the past two. During his military career he had amassed a fortune of fifty thousand pounds and was now considering retirement.

Phoebe glanced up at first with little interest; Mr. Gerard always annoyed her with his overly friendly manner. She forced herself to acknowledge his irritating sociability, but when she looked up again, it startled her to see the stately admiral studying her.

"Forgive me Mr. Gerard, I am afraid I was deep in thought." She politely curtsied to Weatherby. "How do you do Sir?"

"Charmed I'm sure Miss Phoebe," he bowed.

A moment before, she had preferred to wallow in her sorrows, but a second look at the tall, ruggedly appealing man in his mid forties quickly changed her mind. *He's certainly more noble than handsome with his suntanned face. Indeed, he is rather distinguished looking with that hint of gray at his temple and in his sideburns.* While unconsciously studying the Admiral, without thinking Phoebe popped a bite of pork pie in her mouth. When she swallowed, it went down the wrong way and she started to gag. She quickly reached for her glass.

"My dear Miss Phoebe, are you all right?" Mr. Gerard asked.

"Agh, yes, yes, I seemed to have choked on a little bit of something. I will be fine." She hacked indelicately and managed to catch her breath exhaling with, "Yes, I'm fine, thank you."

"Admiral Weatherby is staying with us while on leave from Brighton. Your brother and I thought perhaps he would enjoy this evening."

"Indeed," she replied with a little cough.

As a rule, Phoebe regarded the militia beneath her. *A lady of my rank and fortune, despite that it comes from the trade, does not need to associate with officers in hopes of catching a husband. However, given that Mr. Ramsay has not shown the slightest bit of interest in me this evening, I believe I will not shun the attentions of this admiral. Militia or not, I suppose I should be honored that he has singled me out.*

Phoebe Vance had piqued Weatherby's interest, not by her looks of course, but most particularly because she did not fall all over him. Being in uniform generally caused women to crowd around, and he didn't like that. Her lack of beauty did not concern him; it was the

Admiral's personal opinion that a woman such as Phoebe had to work harder at doing things better than most. His experience generally showed that homely women were superior card players. Next to the Navy, he liked playing whist and was always on the look out for a good partner, preferably a woman. *Indeed, after cards what is a man to do with another man but play more cards and drink?*

"Would you do me the honor of dancing the next set with me?" he asked.

"Why yes, thank you," she smiled, affectedly. "I'd be pleased."

As they danced their second set, Weatherby broke the silence, "Miss Phoebe, would you allow me to call on you tomorrow?"

"I would regard it an honor sir."

He smiled with reserve and asked further, "Might I inquire, do you indulge in whist?"

"Yes, I am quite fond of the game." She wanted to cry, she was so relieved that she had not ended up a wallflower at the ball, which she'd begun to believe she would be.

"I will look forward to several games," he replied, with a tone of superiority in his voice and austerity in his posture, which Phoebe did not notice.

Dancing most sets with Louisa throughout the evening gave great pleasure to David Tristam. *She is so beautiful in her lavender and lace gown,* he thought, *and when we dance, she moves like a silk scarf in a gentle breeze.* As he went for refreshment in between sets, he thought about their time together over the past two weeks; he had asked to call on her nearly every day.

Each time he asked, he loved to tease her when she replied with, "Of course Mr. Tristam, you know how my mother takes pleasure in serving you tea, and my father so enjoys talking with you."

"What about you Miss Louisa?" he would say. "I come not only to see your mother and father, but to see how you are doing as well." She seemed flustered by his response and he enjoyed watching the color rise in her cheeks. Then he would change the subject.

The day before he had asked her to walk into town with him,

"There are a couple of books I would like to pick up at Dillard's. Would you and Harriett do me the honor of walking with me?"

As the three of them finished their business in Broomfield and headed home, David and Louisa strolled side by side, wrapped up in their own reverie of unspoken feelings for each other. When they approached the middle of the bridge, as Harriet lagged behind talking with a friend, Louisa looked over the side.

"I wish we had brought some bread crumbs to feed the ducks," she mused brushing a wisp of hair from her forehead.

"They are delightful to watch, aren't they? Perhaps the day after tomorrow, we can come back and do as you like," David said studying her countenance; more and more each day he relished seeing her and regretted having to bid her good evening.

As they danced the last set at the Glenvalley Ball, David asked if he could see Louisa in the morning. "I have something very particular I would like to speak to you about."

"Of course, Mr. Tristam," she replied, having to take a deep breath to control the excitement she felt. *It can only mean one thing,* she thought, *but I dare not speak of it.* "Why don't you come by at ten thirty?"

"That will be perfect," he said with a twinkle in his eyes.

The next morning Louisa awoke full of excitement as she stretched and yawned; she had scarcely been able to sleep because of David and the ball the night before. She pulled on her blue velvet robe thinking, *I hope with all my heart that he plans to propose. To be married to a man I truly love and who is also as rich and handsome as a prince; could it really happen to me?* She stepped over to her vanity to look at herself in the mirror. *In case I'm wrong, I am glad I did not say anything to anyone. It is nine o'clock now and he will be here in an hour and a half, it's still plenty of time to groom and dress.*

At that moment there came a knock on her bedroom door. "A letter for you, Miss Louisa," Hanna, one of the Stuart's servants said, opening the door ajar. "Mr. Tristam brought it by and asked if he could see you. Of course, I said you were still sleeping, but that I would bring the letter right up."

Louisa's heart sank. "Thank you Hanna. Leave me now, please." She breathed deeply and read to herself.

Dear Miss Louisa,

Please accept my sincerest apologies for having to postpone our visit today. At dawn I received an urgent post from Bristol regarding a business matter of great importance; my immediate attention is required. My man and I will ride there and back as fast as we possibly can and should return by Tuesday week.

Please know that with all my heart there is nothing I wanted more than to speak with you today, but for now I will have to endure the wait until my return.

Most fondly, David Tristam

Louisa fought her tears of disappointment. *I don't know if I shall be able to bear his absence, but there is nothing to be done for it.*

"If only Hanna had come to get me," she sighed heavily and wiped a tear from her cheek.

She was determined to endure her frustration silently and gently laid his note under her pillow. After dressing, she went downstairs to have breakfast with her family, all the while trying to maintain a smile.

"Louisa," her mother intoned loudly, "Hanna tells me you had a letter this morning. I heard horses outside my window and looked to see Mr. Tristam and his man riding away. What did his letter say and where pray tell is he going?"

"Now wife," Mr. Stuart scolded, "I'd say that is none of your affair." He smiled at Louisa. "Dear daughter, you need not tell her anything if you don't wish to."

"It's all right Father," she smiled lovingly. "He was called away to Bristol for several days. That is all."

"Well you cannot fool me, Miss Louisa. I see that you are downhearted. But never mind, I know about matters like this," her mother chortled at her own perspicacity. "Mark my words; he will be back as quickly as possible and will propose. You wait and see. I saw him last night with you, dancing all those sets. He's in love."

"Mrs. Stuart, that is quite enough! Leave the poor girl alone." Her father got up and patted Louisa on the shoulder. "Never mind child, your mother has good news that will cheer you up."

"What is it Mother? Please tell me."

Harriet answered, "It's Gabriella. She and Mr. Newton sent a post right after Mr. Tristam left. They should be arriving here this afternoon from London."

"Yes," Mrs. Stuart cooed. "Your twin sister will be here by supper time. Oh how I've missed her this past year. I'll have Cook prepare a goose."

"That's wonderful," Louisa sighed, happy for the diversion. "I too have missed her." She finished her breakfast in hopes that she would stop worrying about seeing David again. When she went into the parlor she saw an ugly hat on the table and decided redecorating it would take her mind off her worries for awhile. "I think I will just fix this up as a gift to Gabriella."

Chapter 17

A week after the Glenvalley ball in cool but pleasant weather, Veronica and Colette took the barouche over to Hedgerow to say good bye to Gabriella. She and her husband had been there for only six days, and much to everyone's dismay they planned to return to Plymouth early the next morning.

Gabriella had changed since her marriage to Mr. Newton. Clearly she was not as happy as she had been before her elopement; in addition she had put on some weight. She used to be full of energy, talking and laughing all the time, but now she had very little to say and no longer bubbled with enthusiasm. Her husband ignored her, not the way men discount their wives when they take them for granted; he did so with veiled contempt.

"I'm so pleased you could come by before we leave tomorrow." Gabriella smiled and turned to her husband, "Don't you agree Mr. Newton that it was good of them to stop over?"

"Indeed it was. Now your father and I are going riding," he said curtly and without further ado left the room.

Had he been more pleasant and thoughtful towards others, he might have been regarded as handsome. However, given to meanness all his life, he had become hateful towards everyone that did not serve a purpose for him. When Gabriella first met him, she had fallen in love instantly and never saw his disguise until it was too late. Despite his reprehensible behavior she loved him none the less.

Though her sisters could see his scorn, their mother seemed quite unmindful of it. Gabriella, by her sad countenance, appeared resigned to it. It was obvious to Veronica and Colette that she was sorry to be going so soon, as she had told them how much she had looked forward to her visit.

"In Plymouth," Gabriella confided to Veronica and Colette, "I spend a great deal of time alone, while Mr. Newton gallivants about town spending money we do not have. I am left to manage the bill collectors." She put her hand to her forehead and sighed, "It has been horrible living so far away. Once when I confronted Mr. Newton about his whereabouts, he harshly reminded me that I was a married woman. I was not to be asking questions that were none of my affair, he said, and then he ordered me to stay home and take care of my duties there."

"Such abuse," Veronica replied. "I'm horrified, but I trust he never struck you?"

"No, his brutal tone of voice was enough that I did not dare broach the subject again. He only allowed us this trip because I threatened to come without him and report his behavior to Father. I know how Mr. Newton respects his good opinion. I believe that alone made him yield to my longings to see my family again."

"Perhaps the fact that he never had a father of his own to look up to is the reason he values our father's high opinion." Veronica said, noting a distinct sadness in Gabriella's countenance and acceptance of her plight. "Oh Gabriella, I'm so happy that you were able to come and visit."

"It's wonderful to be home again," she sighed nervously, folding and unfolding her small hands. "I think I shall be very sorry to return to Plymouth. I do have a few friends there, but with no children yet,

I have time on my hands and I've been determined to read more. Also, I've developed a fondness for song writing and helping out at the vicarage. Mr. Newton and I attend church regularly, but during the week I assist the vicar and his wife with the needy and sick in town."

"Mother said you wrote about your work there and she was quite proud of you for it," Colette remarked.

"I'm sorry dear Gabriella, but we must be going," Veronica sighed. "We said we would be home before dark. Please promise me you will write and that you'll come and visit." She gave her a hug and slipped her a hundred pound note, and whispered, "I'll send you a little more next month."

Gabriella wiped a tear from her eye as she put the money in her pocket. "Thank you Veronica, thank you. I would adore coming to visit and maybe help you with the twins when they're born. I'll write, I promise."

As they got up to leave, Hanna, one of the Stuarts' housemaids barged into the room screaming incoherently. "Mr. Newton's horse," she stammered, "Mr. Newton's horse——, we saw Mr. Newton's horse throw him," she cried out trying to catch her breath. "The horse stumbled when it jumped the hedge crossing the lane."

Another servant burst through the door. "Master Stuart sent me, he said to fetch the doctor and for you to come right away Mrs. Newton." The two servants rubbed their hands together and anxiously wiped their aprons. "It looks very bad, very bad indeed," Hanna said.

"That will be enough," Veronica scolded them gently. "Hanna, see if you can be useful here; Mother is swooning."

Gabriella dashed outside; Colette and Veronica followed as quickly as they could. Louisa sent the other servant for the doctor, and Harriet ran for John Boswell, who was visiting the new young vicar, Roger Witherspoon. At that moment Gavin and Basil rode up.

Mr. Stuart was bent over Mr. Newton when Gabriella reached them. She stood silently staring at her immobile husband for several moments; tears began to stream down her face. The bloody gash in his forehead caused her heart to pound as she knelt beside him.

"Oh Thomas, I'm here," she whispered softly. "Everything will be all right, you'll see. Just lie still, the doctor is on his way."

He put his hand on her cheek and she wept. "I'm sorry it is ending like this my love," he gasped for air. "It is best for you. I was never any good as a husband, but I did love you. Please say you forgive me."

"Oh Thomas, I never stopped loving you." She put her head on his chest and felt him take his last breath. "No, no, please, don't die!" she sobbed, but he could not hear her.

Mr. Stuart put his arm around his daughter and comforted her with tears of his own. Colette and Veronica were overcome with sorrow at the heartbreaking scene. The doctor came, looked for a pulse and then closed Mr. Newton's eyes. Mr. Stuart helped Gabriella to her feet and they went inside with the doctor.

Impassioned by the sight of Mr. Newton and her sister's broken heart, Colette fainted into Basil's arms. He carried her into the house and waited for the doctor to finish seeing to Gabriella and her mother.

"Mr. Newton was unable to withstand the blow to his head," the doctor said to Mr. Stuart. "I have done all I can for his widow and your wife. I think you sir, should take some brandy while I have a look at Mrs. Vance."

Colette began to rouse and sat up with effort, as the doctor felt her pulse. "I'm sorry to be so much trouble," she said, "but may I have a glass of water please?"

"You may," the doctor replied. "Then it is imperative that you return home and take your rest for two days. We don't want all this anxiety to cause you to deliver your child ahead of schedule. Make haste now to peace and quiet. I'll see to your family here for awhile. Then I'll drop over later and check on how you're doing."

Basil rode with Colette and Veronica in the carriage, while Gavin rode his own horse. About half way back to Glenvalley, Colette suddenly doubled over, groaning in pain.

Veronica opened the carriage window and shouted, "Stop the coach!"

"Whatever is the matter darling?" Gavin entreated, jumping down from his horse.

"Colette does not look well at all! Will you ride with us?"

When Gavin stepped into the carriage, he saw there was not much he could do except watch as Colette writhed in agony. "It is as the doctor feared. There is no stopping her pains now; they were most probably triggered by the tragedy of Mr. Newton's death."

Once when Gavin was traveling with just his manservant several years earlier, they had happened upon a carriage stopped in the middle of the road. The woman inside was delivering her child with the help of her befuddled husband. Gavin had helped them as his own servant stood by unable to stomach the sight. Recalling that time, Gavin prayed that Colette could wait to give birth.

"I doubt the doctor will arrive in time, her pains are coming too rapidly." He jumped down from the carriage and ordered one of his footmen to take Basil's horse and fetch the doctor at Hedgerow. "Make haste, man and tell him, but not in front of the others, that Mrs. Vance is likely to have her child before he arrives. Hurry now and don't delay!"

"Darling, I need you to tear me off pieces of your underskirt," Gavin instructed Veronica. "And you man," he shouted to the second footman, "stand by in case you're needed."

Unable to keep the baby from coming, Colette screamed and clung to Basil. Veronica went back into the oversized carriage and helped hold Colette while Gavin did what he could to facilitate the delivery. Colette let out a blood curdling scream, as he took the child's head in his hands. At the same moment Basil fainted. Veronica shoved him out of the way as best she could; Gavin ignored him and with a little prayer and lots of concentration he managed to focus on the task at hand. At length, after several more hair-raising shrieks the baby was born.

Gavin gently laid the child on Colette's stomach but left the cord attached for the doctor to finish. Colette smiled for a brief moment and then fell unconscious. Veronica was covering the child with her torn petticoat as the doctor arrived. Just then Basil roused to semiconsciousness and saw Colette motionless with the baby lying on her stomach.

"Oh no," he wailed, trying to stand up. "She's dead!"

"Calm yourself dear friend," Gavin said. "She is only asleep."

"But the baby, the baby," he moaned, rising up from the carriage floor.

The doctor and Gavin tried to pull Basil out of the way, but to no avail. Gavin gave him a right cross to the chin and knocked him out.

"Here man," Gavin motioned to the footman. "Move him so the doctor can get inside."

With Basil out of the way, the doctor quickly examined the fair haired baby on Colette's stomach. He cut the cord, slapped its bottom and handed the howling child to Veronica.

"Mother and child are going to be fine," he whispered after checking over Colette.

When he stepped out of the carriage he shook Gavin's hand. "You did an excellent job Lord Hunter. Shall we see to the father now?" He chuckled and reached out to help Basil, who had just started to get up. "Congratulations, Mr. Vance, you are the father of a beautiful baby boy."

Still hazy, Basil rushed in to see his wife.

"Oh Basil," Colette cried, tears running down her cheeks, "isn't he perfect!"

Basil grinned from ear to ear. "I'm so proud of you. He is beautiful. Thank you for making me the proudest father in the world." He bent over his wife and child and kissed them each on the forehead. "Thank you, thank you. I love you both so much."

Once out in the fresh air, the doctor watched Veronica as Gavin enfolded her in his arms. "Mrs. Vance told me of your condition Mrs. Hunter," the doctor said noticing her ashen color. "You must return to Glenvalley post haste where you are to remain in bed for two days." He turned to Gavin. "She's to have absolutely no excitement!"

"I will see to it sir," Gavin said holding Veronica close. "Come dear, we'll ride in the carriage together and get you and your sister home immediately."

Gavin helped her up, recalling that it had taken him a month to conquer his feelings of nausea after assisting the frantic husband deliver his wife's baby. The thought of his own twins being born made him start, and suddenly he felt a strange sensation. *I cannot fathom the pain of having one child; having two is more than I can envision. What is worse, it will be my own wife suffering and by this I am greatly disturbed.*

After settling in their rooms, Veronica and Gavin supped lightly on bread, apples and cheese and a glass of wine. Afterwards, she went right to bed and immediately fell into a deep sleep. Later Geeves helped Gavin with his bath and had some brandy brought up.

In the middle of the night Veronica woke up screaming. "Oh Gavin," she cried, "I dreamed I was all alone on the moor delivering the twins. You weren't there and no one would help me. It was awful."

"It's all right darling, I'm here." He comforted her until she fell back to sleep.

She did not wake again until noon the next day. While she slept Gavin went downstairs to check on Colette, Basil and the baby. Upon his return he saw that Veronica was in her boudoir. Margaret opened the door to his knock.

"Would you ask my wife if I could see her alone please?" he asked.

Veronica overheard him, "It's all right Margaret, please leave us."

Gavin took her hand and asked, "How are you feeling darling? You look extraordinarily beautiful this morning. I was however, concerned for you last night. Except for the dream, you slept so soundly that I feared you would never wake up."

"Please don't worry about me, I am quite well. I just want to know how Colette and the baby are. Have you seen them yet today?"

He smiled thinking of the newborn. "Yes, they're doing fine and the baby is perfect, clearly a miracle. They are anxious for you to see him. Though Basil is mortified by his helplessness yesterday, I have assured him to think nothing of it. What we went through was trying for everyone."

"I am so proud of you. If you had not been there I don't think I could have managed. I wonder how my family is enduring. Surely they've heard about the baby?"

"I will write a note and have a servant take it to them if you like," Gavin said. "By the way they are naming the child Charles Gavin after Basil's father and after me for helping deliver him." Gavin chuckled, "I am quite honored."

"That's very thoughtful of them darling, I am so pleased." She stretched and ran her fingers through her long curls. "Remember in your message to Hedgerow to let them know the baby's name. Now would you have Margaret come back in now, please; I need to dress."

Gavin frowned. "The doctor said you were to remain in bed until tomorrow, but I can see by the determined look on your face that you will have your way."

"Please don't worry darling. I feel fine, really; and I do so want to see Colette and the baby. There is no other way of doing it, for she is less fit than I to be up and about. I promise to stay dressed just long enough to see them both. Then I'll return to our room. Will you allow me this one indulgence?" she pleaded, knowing he would.

"I suppose I cannot stop you, but please, I must insist on coming with you."

Veronica smiled to herself. She loved it when he conceded to her wishes without argument. She did not generally go against him, but sometimes, like now, he could not have persuaded her to do otherwise.

When he left, Margaret came in and Veronica related to her what had happened the day before. "Of course, I'm sure you heard all about it," Veronica said with a sigh. "And even though Mr. Newton was not the most pleasant of men, he did not deserve to die. It was a terrible thing."

"Indeed, my lady. It must have been quite difficult as well to have helped your sister deliver her child."

"Oh Margaret, everything happened so fast, I don't remember much."

"Perhaps that's just as well, my lady. I'm certain the only pleasant thing to remember is her beautiful little boy."

"Certainly, this is true," Veronica replied. "You know I was very impressed with my little sister, Gabriella. Upon seeing her again after a year, it was obvious to me that her marriage was not a happy one. Nevertheless, she loved her husband, despite his faults. I have to admire her for that. I think perhaps she really has changed from the silly, foolish girl she was a year ago."

Chapter 18

A week after Charles Gavin Vance was born Mr. and Mrs. Stuart took the carriage to Glenvalley with Louisa, Harriett and Gabriella to see the baby. It was as joyous an occasion as possible under the circumstances. Gabriella mourned her husband's death, not because she would miss him; in truth she was relieved to be free of him. Her sorrow was for the person she always thought him capable of becoming, as well as remembering how much she had adored him when they eloped. She would not say these things to her family, but instead played the dutiful and properly saddened wife.

When Veronica asked how she was managing, Gabriella replied, ogling over baby Charles, "This is a time to rejoice. I'm the only one who needs to mourn, and I can do that in private. Notwithstanding this, my happiness at the thought of a new addition to our family does a great deal to help push away the cloud of regret overhead. Furthermore, I am pleased to tell you that I'll be staying on at Hedgerow for awhile."

"That's wonderful dear," Veronica said. "When will you return to Plymouth?"

"I may just send for my things and never go back. I don't have to hide the fact that I wasn't happy there." Gabriella sighed and brushed a wisp of her blond hair from her pretty face. "To be home again and near the ones I love is most gratifying to me. Maybe after awhile I'll sail for the Americas. I have thought about it often but have never made any plans."

"I certainly hope you won't jump into that decision without a great deal of thought," Colette admonished. "I love the idea of you living nearby to visit with Charles and me once all our sisters have gone away and married." She laughed and smiled down at her newborn. "He is such a joy."

"I promise I won't do anything rash. You know between my five hundred and the thousand pounds a year from Mr. Newton's estate, which I understand I shall have, there will be plenty of money to do with as I like." Gabriella smiled; *he might have been a rat most of the time, but at least he did not leave me destitute,* she thought, though she would not dream of saying such a thing out loud.

Louisa had longed to hear from David Tristam, but since he had neither returned nor written to date, she was grateful for the occupation of tending to her sisters. This mainly consisted of spending time with Gabriella and keeping her spirits up as well as visiting with little Charles, and Veronica before she returned to Ivywood. These things helped immeasurably to keep Louisa's mind off David each day. Even so, every night in the privacy of her bedroom she prayed that he would come back soon, or at least write to her.

On Tuesday, three weeks to the day since David's departure, Louisa and her sisters returned home from a visit to Glenvalley. Louisa saw David's majestic, white horse tied to the post in front of the house. And as if that were not enough to make her heart beat fast, it surprised her to see him enjoying a cup of tea in the parlor with her mother and father.

When she entered the room, he stood, balancing his tea cup in one hand, and bowed. "Mrs. Newton, Miss Louisa, Miss Harriet, what a delight to see you. Your mother assured me you would be home within the hour and insisted that in the meantime I take tea."

Louisa curtsied and felt the color in her cheeks rise high, right along with the butterflies in her stomach. "Mr. Tristam, it was kind of you to call."

"I could do no less. After all, I am long overdue based on what I said in my letter when I left. On my journey to Bristol and back, I thought often of seeing your roses again. I wonder Miss Louisa if you would walk with me in your garden."

She looked at her mother, "Do you need me for anything just now?"

"Of course not, by all means you two must walk together in the garden."

With this assurance and a nod from her father, Louisa and David went out to the Stuart's small, but beautifully maintained, park. Upon entering it David went right to the Yellow roses and cut one with his pocket knife.

"I believe you once told me you prefer the yellow rose to all others. Do you mind if I put this on my coat?"

"Please do," she smiled nervously. "And yes, the yellow rose is my favorite of the roses, but in truth, my most beloved flower in the whole world is the gardenia. Its fragrance, I believe, is beyond compare."

"I saw the gardenias when we entered the park."

"Well it is too bad we did not cut one of those for your coat. But I have an idea," Louisa smiled. "Why don't we take the yellow rose into the house and you take the gardenia for yourself? Mother will think I am quite silly, but it does not matter."

"I know, I will keep the yellow rose, and you can put the fragrant gardenia in your hair." David laughed, "And then what will your mother think?"

"Mother will have plenty to say, and surely my sisters will laugh and call me a gypsy."

Next to the lush white gardenias Louisa sat down on a wooden bench as David cut the gardenia and slipped it behind her ear. The next thing she knew, he was on bended knee staring up at her with his persuasive green eyes.

"Miss Louisa, you don't look at all like a gypsy. I must be bold and declare that you are more beautiful then I even remembered the whole while I was in Bristol. I thought of nothing but you during my absence and longed to be back here at Hedgerow with you."

Surely he can see my heart beating through my dress, she thought, putting her hands to her face. *If not that then he cannot help but see that my face is on fire. I feel like I shall faint for this emotion welling up in me.*

"Louisa," he whispered her name tenderly. "You must know that I love and adore you. Will you marry me dearest, loveliest Louisa?"

"Mr. Tristam, David, I, I am—" *Is this really happening? This is all I've thought of for weeks, no months, though I was afraid to believe it.* "Oh David, I—," tears began to run down her flushed cheeks.

"Darling, what do these tears mean? Can it be that you don't love me?" His striking eyes reflected sadness, but his square jaw showed determination as he removed his gloves. "No, of course you love me. I know you do because I feel it. You love me like I love you with all your heart." He kissed her hand and then took his handkerchief to dab her cheeks. "Why are you crying my love?"

"Oh David, I love you more than I can say; I just find it difficult to understand why you would want to marry someone like me. I have no fortune and no connections."

"My darling Louisa, just remember that after we are wed, you will have connections and riches of which few can imagine. There, it is settled. Now will you say that you'll marry me?"

Her tears continued to flow. "If you are certain this is not a dream then I will consent to be your wife. But! You must first vow to love and cherish me until I die. I could not bear to have a husband who might not love me always."

"Is that what this is all about? Did you think I would not love you forever? My dearest darling, you have my pledge that I shall care for you with my very soul, so long as I draw breath. Truly, I love you more than life." He pulled her into his arms and kissed her with deep emotion.

She sighed, reveling in his embrace as she murmured in barely a whisper, "I do love you, I do, and I want to be your wife."

He held her by her shoulders and leaned back to gaze into her soft brown eyes. "And as my wife, we will see the world together. I've known since Twelfth Night at Ivywood that I wanted to spend the rest of my life with you."

She giggled, and her sweet smile enchanted him. "How could you know such a thing?"

"I know lots of things my beloved and soon to be wife."

"Surely, I'm the most privileged girl in all of England to have your love. Most certainly, there will be many broken hearts and tongues wagging at the news of you taking a country wife. And I will be the envy even of my sisters." She glowed with happiness as she stood up. "I can't wait to tell them, though I have little doubt they'll be surprised. And my mother, she will be ecstatic. Will you speak to Father now so that I can share my joy?"

David chuckled. "I hope you'll forgive me, my beautiful Louisa, but I spoke to your father while you and your sisters were at Glenvalley. He has accepted my offer for your hand, with the understanding, of course, that you agree." He kissed her again, with even greater fervor than before. "I trust you do agree?" He smiled handsomely and reached for her hand to kiss her finger tips.

She nearly swooned, reeling from the effects of his touch. "You know I do!"

"Why don't I see you to the door then I can return to Glenvalley and settle in. Would it be all right if I called on you again first thing in the morning?"

"Of course, and please plan to join us for breakfast, we eat at nine thirty. I will hardly bear the evening without your presence. I'm so happy."

"I shall think of nothing but my love for you the entire night," he said as he kissed her tenderly on the mouth. "Nine thirty tomorrow morning will be perfect." He waved and rode off on his white horse, looking back once to blow her a kiss.

Mrs. Stuart and Louisa's sisters happened to be looking out the window when they saw David leave. Then one look at the smile on Louisa's face and they could not keep still.

"Now mother, Gabriella, Harriet, calm yourselves please while I tell you my news. Mr. Tristam and I are engaged. I am so happy; I can scarcely believe it's true."

"I knew it, I knew it," Mrs. Stuart blurted out, "Did I not tell you it was so. Oh dearest Louisa, I'm so proud of you." She turned to Harriet. "Run and get your father. I want Louisa to share her happy news with him."

"But Mother he knows," Louisa laughed. "Mr. Tristam asked him earlier before we returned home. You needn't bother him Harriet."

"Oh yes she does. You go and bring him here," her mother ordered. "I must scold him for not telling me. Besides we should all share in your joy together. Just wait until I tell Mrs. Gerard. She'll be pleased, as well as a bit envious that it is not her Sarah who is to be married."

Mr. Stuart entered the room and put his arm around Louisa. "Well Louisa, I know you will be very happy. Mr. Tristam is a find young man, and I heartily approve."

"And when will the wedding be?" Mrs. Stuart interrupted.

"We have not set a date yet, but we will tomorrow. Now I must send a note over to Veronica and Colette to give them my good news. After all, Veronica and Mr. Hunter are leaving in the morning. I doubt that I'll be seeing them again until Harriet's wedding."

"Well do as you wish Louisa," her mother chuckled. "I know your sisters will be most pleased to hear of your engagement to one of the richest men in England."

Chapter 19

Audrey Hunter and James Farnsworth had seen each other only once since the holidays, but they wrote nearly everyday. When they met again at Ivywood for their engagement party, they were inseparable.

"I have missed you so much Audrey. If not for your letters I should have perished for want of seeing you." James smiled and held her cherub face in his hands. "You did get my sister's note, didn't you? Your brother will permit you to come back with me to Bath? My sister and I will be most desolate if you cannot attend us."

"Of course dear James, my brother has said I may return with you and stay the entire month of June. Then I will leave for my aunt's in London, and when the twins are born I'll come back here for the Christening." Audrey looked up at him with eager blue eyes. "You can come here then as well and also be our guest for Twelfth Night again this year. And lest I forget, my aunt in London has extended her invitation to you and asks that you accept her apologies for keeping me to herself these past months. You will come and visit me in

London before the Christening, won't you?"

"There is no doubt. And I will do all in my power from now on to prevent us from being apart for more then a week at a time until we are married," James said. "You have made me very happy with this news. Now I want you to tell me how much you love me, for such sweetness from your lips is music to my ears."

"I do love you James, I do," she said, suddenly feeling shy, as his steady gaze upon her made her feel self-conscious.

He gathered her in his arms and kissed her passionately as he twirled her around. "It's wonderful to see you," he sighed. "But I think it's time to go inside and be sociable, don't you?"

She agreed, and took his arm as they walked back to the manor.

Two days later, on the first Thursday in May the sun shined brightly for Audrey and James' engagement party. It was held outdoors in the perfectly manicured gardens where the green grass smelled freshly cut, and the fragrant roses were in full bloom. A huge canopy, placed between the dining terraces and the front lake, sheltered a banquet of food.

Among the Hunter's many friends and acquaintances present were Phoebe Vance and Admiral Thomas Weatherby, who she had met at the Glenvalley Ball. "No, dearest Ursula," Phoebe said to her sister as they walked toward the house together, "It is too soon for professions of love and marriage, but I feel certain they will come."

"Well, I surely hope it will not be long. I can only imagine that you are eager to set up house for yourself," Ursula replied. "I have to admit though that the Admiral clearly does not seem to be in any hurry."

Indeed, there is no need to rush, Weatherby thought as he overheard the sisters talk. *For the time being I am content to simply court her.* Unlike Miss Phoebe, he did not care whether people liked him or not, and it was this very disregard for the opinion of others that drew them to him. Striving for approval that was not easily forthcoming was Phoebe's most ardent pursuit; occasionally Thomas gave his. However, he was still undecided about whether or not to propose, as he was determined not to make a rash decision about such a grave matter.

Captain Bradford and Lillian Ramsay were also among the invited guests. They stood away from the crowd talking under the shade of an elm tree by the lake. It was since the Glenvalley ball that they had last spoken, but their correspondence had been weekly and echoed hints of affection for each other.

"Lillian, my dear cousin, may I speak to you freely?" Douglas asked.

"Of course," she smiled broadly at him, "after all we're good friends, are we not?"

"Yes we are, and I've been thinking a lot about you since the Glenvalley Ball but particularly after Mr. Newton's death. My thoughts cause me to leave caution to the wind in a certain matter, for who can say what tomorrow will bring." He paused and cleared his throat, "I love you Lillian. I have known for sometime and have thought of little else. I want you for my wife but have been concerned about asking so soon after your mother's death. Notwithstanding this, I can wait no longer. Will you consent dearest, loveliest Lillian to be my wife?"

She was astonished by his confession and could not answer him right away. *I did not expect this to come so soon.*

"Does your reticence mean that I am to be rejected?" he asked looking distressed.

"I don't know what to say Douglas. Will you give me a moment, please?" she pleaded, not wanting to say yes or no.

While contemplating her reply, she looked over his shoulder and was shocked to see a huge lion, with mane fully fanned, darting through the grounds. Three men wielding whips and one carrying a musket chased after it. It happened so fast that many guests did not notice the melee at first, but those who did started screaming and running to get out of the lion's path. Panicked and speechless, Lillian pointed at the beast and started to run, but Douglas took her in his arms and held her tight.

"Don't move or make a sound," he whispered. "It is not coming at us, and we don't want to draw his attention over here."

Those chasing the animal tried to divert it from the canopy of food, but it advanced straight towards the crowd gathered there. Gavin, Veronica and the Admiral stood next to a table brimming with roast beef and other delights, when suddenly they noticed the beast charging directly at them. Gavin quickly reached for a carving knife from one of the meat platters. His heart pounded furiously, and then he saw Admiral Weatherby grab Veronica out of the way just in time.

A fraction of a second later, the lion leaped for Gavin. He instinctively jumped backwards and drove the knife into the creature's chest. Just as quickly Gavin rolled out of the way as the lion plunged toward the ground, landing its eight-foot, spread eagle form on the entire table of food, where the two, as one, crashed to the earth.

Gavin caught his breath, as the lion tamer dashed up to the lion and fired a shot through its head.

"Just want to make sure," the tall, swarthy man said, offering Gavin his hand to help him up from where he had landed just inches from the dead beast.

Veronica put one hand on her heart and the other over her mouth, gasping and feeling faint. The admiral's strong arms supported her and his words of encouragement gave her strength.

"It's all right now Lady Hunter. Your husband is safe. Let's have a look."

They walked over to Gavin. Veronica recoiled at the sight of the bloody beast mingled with the destruction it had caused. In shock, she found her voice and with it came tears.

"Gavin are you all right?"

"Don't cry darling, I'm fine, though a little shaken I will admit." He put his arm around her. "I believe we owe the Admiral here a debt of gratitude for taking you out of harms way just in time." He bowed to Weatherby, "Thank you sir that was good thinking."

"I'd say you are the one with excellent foresight. That knife saved your life," Weatherby said. "I am gratified indeed that you and Lady Hunter are safe." He looked at the circus troop and lion tamer. "Pray tell, you have some explaining to do."

"Please accept our humblest apologies," the lion tamer said. "We are with the circus on our way to Ashbourne from Newhaven. About a mile or two up the road the lion cage hit a small boulder and tipped over. In the process the lock broke and the lion dashed off before we even realized what had happened. At the same time a cage with about twelve monkeys also turned on its side, and they all escaped. Fortunately most of the chimps were being captured as we started after the lion."

"Well we're grateful the lion is no longer a danger to anyone," Gavin said, as everyone turned toward a horrendous cry for help.

Ursula Twackham shrieked as Phoebe tried desperately to rid herself of a monkey that had jumped from the top of the food tent onto her hat. The animal bounced up and down squealing with delight as it played with the large, purple feather that loomed high above Phoebe's hat. She opened her mouth to cry out, but no words came forth. Her straight yellow hair stood on end flying in every direction, while the circus monkey swished the plume back and forth. Finally Phoebe screamed so shrilly that for a moment the monkey went limp, and everyone thought it had died of heart failure. However, only a few seconds passed before the little creature began jumping up and down again, this time dangling the now loose feather in Phoebe's face.

As she made hysterical attempts to rid herself of the pest, the Admiral dashed to help her. Nevertheless, he was stopped short of his target by coming upon Mrs. Twackham, who lay in his path swooning. Her husband, having indulged in too much drink, also blocked the way when he fell on his face as he stooped down to revive his wife.

"See here Twackham," Weatherby said disgustedly, "move aside and allow me to help Miss Phoebe."

One of the lion tamer's men reached Phoebe first and rescued the monkey from harm just as Weatherby got there. "There, there Miss Phoebe," the Admiral said. "There is no more need to panic. Everything is all right now." He patted her arm, feeling uncharacteristically compassionate. "I'm sure this has been most dreadful for you."

"Please don't leave me, Sir." she pleaded with fear of another attack showing in her small narrow eyes.

"You are safe now, but have a look over here," he pointed to the circus men dragging off the dead lion. "You are not the only one today who has had misfortune. You missed Mr. Hunter almost being eaten by a lion. Our host is unhurt, but just look at the destruction the beast has caused."

Phoebe was unprepared for the shock. After one look at the jumble of splintered wood, broken china, crystal and food scattered all over, she started to cry.

"Now my dear," Weatherby said, in a rare display of affection as he put his arm around her. "Everything will be fine. There's no need to cry." He handed her his handkerchief. "Why don't you and your sister go in and freshen up. I'm certain you will feel better once you have done so."

Captain Bradford finally let go of Lillian, and together they walked over to the tent to see what had happened. Lillian was shocked by the chaos she saw and tears came to her eyes. Suddenly she knew what he had said was true.

"Oh Douglas, that could have been you instead of Gavin, and you might not have been as fortunate. I cannot bear the thought," she cried.

"That is what I was trying to say earlier; we can never know what might happen to us." He took her arm and guided her back to the tree where they had enjoyed their earlier privacy. "It's going to be all right now Lillian, you will see."

Without thinking he took her face in his hands and kissed her. The touch of his lips sent a rippling chill through her, and he felt the same spine tingling delight.

She took a deep breath and sighed, "I love you, Douglas. Until now I was unsure of myself. Indeed, I don't know what I should do without you by my side. Even when my mother lived, you were so kind to me, and I looked forward to your visits. Then afterwards you were there for me and now, now I could not bear the thought of being without you."

"Darling, beautiful Lillian, does this mean your answer is yes, you will have me? I love you with all my heart. I have waited so long for such love." He felt gayer than he had in years.

"Oh yes Douglas, I will marry you." She held him close and whispered, "I never want to let you go."

The gala continued well into the evening with food and dancing, despite the unwelcome interruption from the circus. Late that night when everyone had retired for the night, Veronica and Gavin sat in front of the roaring fire in the library and talked over the day's events.

"Even though the lion practically ruined the affair today," Veronica said, "the damage could have been much worse."

Gavin smiled. "It certainly could have been, but I must tell you how proud I am of you. You remained calm through it all. Most women would have gone to pieces; they would have been flat out seeing what you did."

"But dearest, you are the one to be commended," Veronica replied looking up at him, admiring his intense, blue eyes. "There are few men who would be alive to talk about such an experience. In truth I was frightened and horrified, but once I saw you were safe, I could see no reason to act like a silly girl. After all, there was little harm done except to the buffet and everyone's nerves."

"And certainly," he chuckled, "the horror of the lion was offset by the amusement of the monkey dancing around on poor Miss Phoebe's head."

"Clearly," Veronica agreed, "she made more fuss over that little animal than was seen over the lion. Though I did feel sorry for her and would not have liked it if a monkey had jumped on me like that."

Gavin stared at the fire. "I don't know how we can ever thank Admiral Weatherby for his part in saving you from disaster, though he said our gratitude was enough. You know, I believe he is perfect for Miss Phoebe."

"I wonder when he will ask for her hand."

"In his own good time, I'm certain," Gavin assured her. "He's not the sort of man to jump into anything quickly without giving it a great deal of thought, especially marriage to someone like Miss Phoebe.

Perhaps by Christmas he will know all he needs to about her. By then he will have determined whether or not she is worthy of him."

"Well I'm thankful it is not I waiting for you to make up your mind," Veronica laughed. "At her age, I would be quite eager for a proposal, as no doubt she is."

"I was just thinking," Gavin grinned, "poor Miss Phoebe, it is more than her age that keeps her from marrying. Along with her unfortunate lack of physical appeal, her personality leaves a great deal to be desired. I suppose it is well she has a sizable fortune, though so far it has not tempted anyone that I am aware of except the Admiral."

"We should be ashamed of ourselves speaking of one of our guests like that," Veronica's bold, brown eyes twinkled and she could not keep the mirth from her tone. "By the way, did you notice that the Captain seems quite taken with Lillian? I don't think he left her side the entire day."

"As far as I could see, he did not, but we shall know soon enough what they are up to." Gavin put his arm around his wife. "Now let's have no more talk of the day's events. What do you say to the fact that I have once again locked us in our library and there are no servants to disturb us?"

She smiled alluringly at him and snuggled into his arms. "Well, I did tell Margaret not to wait up for me. And may I say that your attention to detail pleases me."

The next day all but family had departed from Ivywood. That evening Veronica and Gavin, along with Audrey, Mr. Farnsworth, Edward, Lillian, and Capt. Bradford enjoyed a quiet supper.

"Dear brother and sister," Audrey said after the main course had been served, "thank you for the most excellent party. It was perfectly delightful to have all my friends and our mutual acquaintances here to celebrate with Mr. Farnsworth and me."

"It was our pleasure to honor your engagement in such a way, my dear sister." Gavin chuckled softly, "However, I do apologize for all the trouble in the garden. Nevertheless, I suppose sometimes that a little excitement, without any real harm, can be good for us, especially just when we think we are invulnerable."

"How right you are cousin." Douglas stood up and reached for Lillian's hand. "That being said, perhaps you would allow me to make an announcement. I have not gone through the proper channels yet, but for that I will ask your forgiveness cousin Edward. You see, Lillian has accepted my offer of marriage."

Edward jumped from his chair and raised his glass. "Here, here, let me be the first to offer a toast to such excellent news. Most assuredly dear cousin, you are forgiven for Lillian has never glimmered with such joy."

"Thank you, thank you all," Douglas beamed. "Now we would like to share with you some of the decisions we have made."

"We would be honored to hear them," Gavin winked at Veronica and smiled knowingly.

"When we are married Lillian is going to quit Lochaven. I told her about the Old Newbury Estate ten minutes down the road, and we took a ride on horseback there this afternoon. It's available, and we are considering it for ourselves. Secondly," Douglas smiled at his intended, "I am going to leave the regiment and become a gentleman of leisure; Lillian has asked this of me. Thirdly, we want to be married with very little ado, a small ceremony, you know, with only immediate family. What with Lady Ramsay's death, and my having little to recommend me, we thought it best if we slipped away and held a private ceremony after the twins are born."

"Naturally, we want to return from our honeymoon in time for Ivywood's Twelfth Night festivities," Lillian added, her blue eyes clear and bright. "In the meanwhile we should be able to have Newbury Park ready to move into by then."

"Lillian, I trust you are in complete agreement with everything?" Edward asked.

"Oh yes, brother. I could not be more pleased."

"It's settled then," Gavin said. "Indeed, you two have been earnest in making plans. Perhaps, Douglas, you would allow me to offer Ivywood chapel for the ceremony, and I am sure Boswell would be pleased to marry you two."

"Lillian, if I can be of assistance in any way," Veronica offered, "please allow me the privilege of doing so. And, I can't tell you how wonderful it will be to have you so near by."

"I am going to miss you at Lochaven, Lillian," Edward said. "If you will permit me, however, as a wedding gift, I would like to pay for all the new furnishings and remodeling necessary for wherever you choose to live. I would be satisfied if you would indulge me this pleasure."

Lillian got up and kissed him on the cheek. Standing next to him she seemed like a little bird, for she was as petite as he was tall and broad. "Oh Edward, you are so dear to me. Thank you for your kindness and generosity. I never believed I could be so happy."

She went over to give Veronica and Audrey a hug. "Thank you for your offers to help too. We will have great fun together as we plan."

"What about your friend Rosemary?" Audrey asked. "Where will she go?"

"She has indicated a desire to travel, and her brother has told her that she may come and live with him at any time she chooses. I will speak with her when we return home. I am certain she will be pleased for me and will have plenty of time to make plans of her own."

The following morning Gavin and Veronica waved goodbye to their family, happy to have time to themselves before they prepared to leave for Hedgerow and her sister Harriet's impending wedding to Boswell the vicar.

Chapter 20

Since the death of her husband, Gabriella Stuart Newton had moved back to Hedgerow where she adored being with her family and friends again. She and Sarah Gerard, their neighbor who was only two years younger, became good friends. They helped out together at the church and enjoyed working with the new young vicar, Roger Witherspoon, who had moved into the parsonage in January.

"Oh Gabriella," Sarah sighed, as they took soup to the home of a sick widow one day, "I think Rev. Witherspoon is very handsome. Don't you agree?"

"Indeed he is Sarah," Gabriella chuckled, something she had done very little of over the past year. "Furthermore, I think he has an eye for you."

"How can you say such a thing, he hardly knows I exist." Sarah, smiled, "Surely though, if you're right, I would not be disappointed."

"Well I know he appreciates our help, as for the other, we'll just have to wait and see. When we get to your place, are you still willing to play for me while I try out the new song I wrote?"

"Of course, I'm always eager to hear what you have written," Sarah said, adjusting her blue bonnet. "But Gabriella, tell me, what do you think of Pastor Witherspoon wanting to walk with us into town tomorrow?"

Gabriella laughed. "I think that it is a little proof of what I just said. And don't forget, he gladly accepted your mother's invitation to tea for the day after tomorrow."

"He did seem to like the idea, didn't he?" Sarah questioned eagerly. "I truly hope you will come with your mother and father."

"I will be there, but after that the remainder of the week will be taken up with getting ready for Harriet's wedding. I am so happy for my sisters. They have made very fortunate alliances and if I never marry again, I should be content to know that they are well."

"What about this evening Gabriella, are you planning on attending?"

"Yes. Colette is expecting all of us at seven, and we will stop by for the vicar as well."

"May I ask you dear friend," Sarah questioned with concern. "How are you bearing up under the loss of your husband?"

"You must understand Sarah; I was much lonelier when I lived in Portsmouth. Mr. Newton was rarely home and I had only a few acquaintances from the church, but here I have family and friends surrounding me. I'm quite content, thank you. Indeed, I could not be happier than when I am in the company of my nephew, and in a few months I shall be an aunt again, twice over."

"I am glad for you then," Sarah smiled. "Now that your sisters are busy with wedding plans, I think I should be quite lonesome if I did not have the opportunity to help you out at the church and be your friend as well."

In June Harriet Stuart and John Boswell were married in a simple ceremony officiated by the new Vicar Witherspoon. Afterwards, they honeymooned in Scotland for a month, and upon their return home, the newlyweds seemed prodigiously happy and well suited for each other. Since they had settled in at the Ivywood vicarage, Harriet visited Veronica nearly everyday during the first two weeks of September, wanting to see how she was holding up while anticipating the birth of the twins. It had become increasingly difficult for Veronica to get around lately and Harriet wanted to help as much as she could.

"I am doing well enough," Veronica said the day before Colette and Basil Vance were to arrive. "I greatly appreciate your visits Harriet and I know that Gavin enjoys seeing John when he comes with you."

"It is the very least I can do sister. It pleases me to think that perhaps I am of some comfort."

"You surely are. Yet, as excited as I am about having twins, I will be glad when I can get around a little easier. I miss being able to bathe of a morning, though fortunately I am able to keep my time open for my daily devotions and other readings I like to do before I get so sleepy I cannot keep my eyes open."

"Well being with child is no easy feat as I see it. No doubt I will follow in your footsteps someday soon." Harriet laughed, "I certainly hope it is sooner than later."

"Before you go Harriet, I wanted to know what you think of Sarah Gerard's engagement to the vicar, Roger Witherspoon?"

"I am happy for her. I think she has made a wise choice."

Veronica smiled. "I am glad for her too, and surely her parents must be thrilled."

"Though they did not oppose the match, she said they had hoped she would marry someone who was better connected and who possessed a greater fortune."

"It is a shame," Veronica sighed, "that mothers want their daughters to marry for money. I am proud of Sarah for listening to her heart."

"I wrote to her and told her how happy I am being married to a vicar." Harriet smiled, "I think it pleased her to hear that I thought happiness was more important than money."

"Indeed," Veronica said, "and it is not like you or she are without means. You are not paupers living solely on love, and besides Sarah now has her own living of two thousand a year."

"I thank the Lord everyday for our blessings too." Harriet stood up to give Veronica a kiss. "I promised John I would walk into town with him this morning. Is there anything you would like me to get for you, a book perhaps? Sarah told me of a very enjoyable one that is just out. It is entitled *Crystal Pines* and is about some cousins from London who sail to America. They each fall in love with an American girl and only one comes back to England."

"It sounds interesting, why don't you pick that book up for me and have Dillard's send us the bill. Thank you Harriet for coming over and thinking of me. We'll see you tomorrow evening for supper with Colette and Basil."

"One more thing," Harriet asked, "Are you finding Miss Martin to your satisfaction? Do you think you made the right choice for your babies?"

"Yes, I am quite satisfied with Mrs. Anderson's decision to hire the young woman to oversee the nursery. She came with excellent qualifications and references."

Harriet chuckled, "She does have that capable look about her. Her undefined shape and sturdiness of foot make her appear grandmotherly, though she is but twenty-nine."

"Miss Martin is neat and tidy in face and body; she walks with the determination of a woman not to be argued with." Veronica smiled, "She reminds me a little of Margaret, and I think she and I will get along very well. Without a lot of direction from me or Mrs. Anderson, she has taken complete charge of everything, from the staff of nursemaids to making the nursery perfect."

Two days later as Veronica sat in her boudoir Margaret knocked and asked if she could come in. "Would you like help getting dressed my lady? I believe you are to meet your sister and her husband on the terrace for breakfast in about an hour, and the Master is waiting for you in your sitting room. I told him I would have you dressed right away."

"Thank you Margaret," she sighed heavily, as the morning sun shined brightly through the window.

"In truth Margaret, I almost feel like I could stay in bed today; I did not sleep all that well last night. However, I am looking forward to spending time with my sister."

When Veronica was dressed, Margaret went out to inform Gavin that she was ready. Over the last two weeks, he had insisted upon coming to get her every morning, as he seemed overly cautious about leaving her alone.

Gavin opened the door and greeted Veronica with a kiss. "Margaret says you are ready to join us. Colette, Basil and baby Charles are waiting." He took her hand. "Here, let me help you up."

"Thank you Darling." She laughed, "I feel like an overstuffed goose."

"Nonsense, you're the most beautiful lady in all of England, and you are about to give birth to our children."

At the moment he said this Veronica doubled over and could not walk. "Oh Gavin," she cried out in pain, holding her swollen abdomen.

Without thinking, he lifted her up and carried her to the birthing room, which was right across the hall from their bedroom. With a panicked look on his face, he managed to say, "I'll fetch the doctor."

Veronica caught her breath as the pain momentarily subsided. "Please send for Margaret; I think you are about to be—" Another contraction made her bite her tongue and tears began to stream down her face.

Gavin thought he was ready for this moment, since he had contemplated it daily the last month, but he was not. Seeing his wife in agony was more than he could bear. Just as he would dash off for help, Margaret met him coming around the corner. Unable to speak, Gavin frantically pointed to the room.

Quickening her step, she knew instinctively what was happening and immediately took full charge. She ordered one servant to attend the father-to-be, another to get boiling water and a third to see to it that the doctor was on his way. Her last order was to fetch Miss Martin and her nursemaids.

Halfway down the hall, Gavin heard a savage scream and dropped to his knees. It seemed only a few minutes since he had gone for help, but in fact an hour had passed. The next thing he knew, his vicar brother-in-law met him on the stairwell and explained that Basil had sent for him.

"Harriet is downstairs with the Vances right now," John said observing the distressed look on Gavin's face. "Don't worry brother; I see this all the time as the women in the parish give birth. Indeed, it is unpleasant to hear and watch, but I assure you it is all in God's hands."

They sat on a blue cushioned bench in the hallway waiting for news. "I'm not certain I can bear to see her in such agony. And why hasn't the doctor arrived yet?" Gavin asked, greatly distressed. "Do you think Margaret needs help?"

Just as Boswell was about to satisfy Gavin that everything would be all right, the doctor came bounding up the stairs. When he opened the door to the room, a deafening scream raised the hair on the back of Gavin's neck. He jumped out of his seat and started for Veronica.

Boswell took hold of his arm. "Let the doctor do his work, Gavin; she will be fine."

Gavin yielded and sat back on the bench, bewildered by all the scurrying up and down the hall. Finally he noticed Basil sitting quietly beside him. Basil could see that his friend was glad for his presence, though Gavin was unable to say so.

After two more hours Gavin, Basil and Boswell heard one long, savage shriek that Gavin believed could wake the dead. He seriously thought he was going to retch, but he refrained with a great amount of effort and concentration. A short while later Margaret stepped into the hall.

"Sir you may come in now," she said.

Gavin's emotions overcame him at that moment, and he could not speak. He choked back tears and held his breath. Finally he let out a deep sigh and walked in to see his wife. Tears streamed down her checks as she held a baby in each arm.

Immeasurably relieved, he took another deep breath and stared down at his wife and children. "They're beautiful," he said running his hands through her tangled curls, "And so are you. I am overwhelmed."

She whispered between her tears, "I understand how you feel. They are perfect, aren't they? Would you like to hold your sons?"

"May I?" he gasped sitting down in a chair by the bed as the nursemaid put a baby in each arm. Speechless and enraptured, the new father smiled at one and then the other, until finally he found the words. "They are amazing, aren't they."

"Yes," she sighed, choking back emotions. "They are one minute apart, and the oldest one in your right arm has a tiny mole behind his left ear."

"You would be Paul then." Gavin cooed, touching the infant's nose with his lips. "Isn't that what we decided to name the oldest?"

"We did and little Edward looks just like him." She smiled, "how will we ever tell them apart but for the spot behind the ear?"

"I suspect that we will have to put them through inspection when we want to make sure who is who," Gavin laughed. "I think your father will be pleased to know that we named Edward after him. I know my father would be honored if he knew we gave our eldest his name."

As Gavin sat staring and admiring the babies, he felt the doctor tap him on the shoulder. "Your wife needs her rest now sir."

"I'm sorry," Veronica spoke softly, "I don't think I can keep my eyes open any longer. I love you Gavin."

"I love you too, my darling. Thank you for our beautiful sons." Gavin handed the babies to the nursemaid and bent to kiss Veronica as she drifted off into a deep sleep.

Miss Martin ushered the nursemaids upstairs, and the doctor followed to further examine the babies. Gavin kissed Veronica on the forehead again and left for the nursery, eager to look more closely at his boys.

A fortnight after the birth of Paul and Edward, Veronica had moved back into their bedroom to be with Gavin. While they awaited the arrival of other family and friends for the twins' christening,

Veronica recuperated by spending as much time as possible with Colette and the babies.

"I'm so glad that my sister and Basil came to stay with us during this time," Veronica said. "It's been wonderful having them here."

"I enjoy Basil a great deal. And I know that Colette and the twins have been very helpful in keeping you entertained since you've been confined to bed."

Veronica frowned. "As far as I'm concerned three weeks is long enough. Next week when everyone arrives the doctor said I could be up for the christening, but I feel perfectly wonderful already. And that brings me to a question," she reached out for Gavin's hand. "Do you think just this once that you and I could go down to the library together for a short while to visit with Colette and Basil this evening? Colette said they have something to tell us, and after all, I have been up and about the room a little already."

"I don't know if that is wise. The doctor said——"

"Oh darling, I promise I feel well enough that a trip down stairs is not going to do me any harm."

"Well, perhaps. But I insist that you allow a couple of the servants to carry you down in a chair." He raised his hand as she tried to protest. "Now not another word, it's either the chair or bed. I don't mean to be so unbending, but I would not want you or I to suffer the consequences of any ill effects you might have by walking the stairs without the doctor's say in the matter."

"Oh Gavin, I love you for your concern, so I'll accept your terms. Will you please let Colette and Basil know that they can expect us in the library at seven? And I will have Margaret inform Miss Martin that we would like Paul and Edward brought downstairs at the same time."

That evening baby Charles kept everyone amused as Veronica and Gavin held Paul and Edward. "Veronica and I want to thank you for attending us all these weeks," Gavin said to Basil. "I hope you are not too tired of being away from home."

"Not at all my friend, if I recall you did us a great favor by helping with the birth of dear Charles," Basil said, tussling his child's blond curls.

"We owe you his life, I'm sure," Colette smiled. "But now dear brother and sister, there is a reason we asked if we could visit together this evening. We have some very special news we want to share with you."

"We just received a post today," Basil announced.

"What is it?" Veronica asked. "Please do not keep us in suspense."

He grinned. "I'll let Colette tell you."

"Do you remember Veronica, when I mentioned in one of my letters that we were considering a property not far from Ivywood?"

"Oh dearest Colette, you don't mean, do you?" Veronica asked excitedly. "Are you really moving closer to us?"

Basil answered, "Yes we are, and it is only thirty miles of good road southwest of here."

"That would be in the Lake District," Gavin said.

"Yes, in Shropshire near Ellesmere," Basil replied. "Of course, it's a small estate of only a thousand acres. They call it Applewood."

"This is such wonderful news," Veronica said.

"Indeed it is," Gavin smiled at his friend. "It will be a great pleasure to have you but two hours from here rather than four. On horseback it will take even less time."

"Well I know a thousand acres is nothing compared to Ivywood, but the hills and dales along with groves of apples trees will suit us just fine. I cannot wait, but we will not be moving until April."

"I dread telling Mother," Colette laughed. "She will not be happy about it. Nevertheless, it will come about, like it or not. It would be best when they come for the christening that we not say a word to her. We can tell Father of course and he will be glad for us."

Basil sipped his brandy. "Colette and I will be leaving the day after the christening."

"We can't tell you how much we have appreciated your company," Veronica smiled. "We shall miss you both, and baby Charles too of course. But let's not talk about your leaving yet." Veronica motioned for the servant. "I think I will have dessert brought in now. I had Mrs. Anderson order up a chocolate cake to celebrate our time down here this evening, and to thank you for coming."

Three weeks after the twins' christening, Edward Ramsay, James Farnsworth, and Audrey came to stay at Ivywood for Douglas and Lillian's wedding. Although, Edward had set craftsmen to work on refurbishing and furnishing Newbury Park Manor for his sister and her husband, it would not be ready until the Bradfords' returned from their honeymoon in Edinburgh and Glasgow Scotland. By then the manor would be completely ready to move into.

Lillian could hardly wait to settle in. "Don't you think our new home will be perfect?" She remarked excitedly to Veronica and Audrey as they watched her maid help her with her pink satin wedding gown.

"It will be wonderful," Audrey smiled delighted with all that Edward was having done to the Newbury estate. "But you seem nervous cousin, are you all right dear?"

I don't know," Lillian laughed through her tears. "I was thinking about mother. She died still bemoaning the loss of Gavin as a son-in-law. She was quite furious that I did not become Lady Hunter. But alas she is no longer my worry, and I have never been happier."

"Indeed, cousin," Audrey encouraged, "I am sure that your mother is smiling down on you this great day. Surely she would be glad to see you so content."

"We are thrilled for you too Lillian," Veronica said. "We're pleased indeed that you will live so near."

While Lillian prepared to walk down the aisle, Gavin, Edward and James Farnsworth stood with Douglas as he took a sip of brandy to calm him. "I'm amazed to feel such excitement," he laughed. "Me, a man formerly in uniform, used to thrills and entertainment from military life, nervous about a wedding?" He paused and wiped his brow. "Thank you all for your support. I've not felt so wonderful in years and the thought of marrying lovely Lillian has put me in very high spirits."

Gavin put his hand on Douglas's shoulder. "I'm sure I can speak for all of us; we wish you well."

"Indeed," Edward chuckled. "See to it man that you keep my sister happy. If it was any one other than you marrying her, I would be concerned." They all laughed as they waited impatiently for Lillian to enter the room.

Chapter 21

The second week in November, one month after Veronica and Gavin attended the Bradford wedding, they traveled to Ivywood for Louisa and David Tristam's big day. The night before the wedding, Louisa waited for her sisters to join her in her room at Hedgerow. She had asked them if they would stay the night with her, as she hoped having them there would ease her premarital jitters. Before they arrived, Louisa sat thinking of the wonderful visits she and David had enjoyed every day for the past two weeks. They talked about how after their wedding they would stay at his London villa, spend the holidays at Ivywood, and from there move into his family's massive estate in Bristol. He would not tell her what he planned for their honeymoon in the spring.

Several days after David had arrived at Glenvalley, Louisa and he walked into town. He had taken her into the most exclusive shop there and purchased an exquisite, pink, floral fan that he saw her admiring. It was enormously expensive, and she had almost fainted when he asked the shopkeeper to give it to her.

"I'm gratified that you are pleased by so little," David smiled. "And here's something more for you." He pressed some folded notes into her hand, "It's for you to use as you please, dearest. I don't ever want you to be without, and there shall be more where that came from."

"Oh David," she sighed staring down at ten one hundred pound notes, "Whatever shall I do with all this money?"

"Don't fret darling," he laughed. "I'm certain that in a very short time you will become quite accustomed to thinking of ways to spend it. Now on our way back to Hedgerow why don't we walk through the park at the edge of town?"

"I love the park," she replied, thinking how envied she was as she watched the townspeople ogle her and David walking down the street.

When they entered the park, David spotted a fallen tree. "Would you like to sit for a few minutes and rest?"

Once they were seated on the log, he drew her into his arms and kissed her with great passion. "I have wanted to do that from the moment I saw you this morning. You are so delightful, and I love you so much."

She turned bright red, feeling blissfully happy but completely undone. At length, she gazed dreamily into his marvelous green eyes and sighed. "I believe I am barely able to contain my joy at the thought of becoming your wife, dearest David. I shall never understand why I am the most fortunate girl in the world."

"Many of my friends will wonder at my good fortune in finding such a delightful bride as you. Few, if any, will ever know anyone as sweet and innocent."

She laughed. "How can you say such a thing? Why wouldn't any of your friends find a silly country girl like me? Clearly, there are plenty of us around."

"First of all none of those things are true about you. Secondly, because of their pride and prejudice against country society, most would deem it beneath them to look."

He sighed and embraced her. She was wholly enraptured by his kiss until she became momentarily distracted by a creepy frog that had jumped from out of nowhere right onto her lap. They were in a woodsy area near a pond where one could hear them croaking, and she realized too late that they were all around. She squealed and jumped up from the log with a continuous brushing of her skirt to be rid of the frog; she believed they were hideous creatures. Unfortunately in her zeal, she lost her balance and fell backwards over the tree stump. As soon as David leaned over to reach for her hand and pull her up, he tripped and landed on top of her. Both of them, and the frog as well, escaped injury, but David and Louisa remained on the ground laughing so hard, neither could move.

When they finally stood up, David gasped, "Oh my darling Louisa, there are grass stains and dirt all over the back of your pretty blue gown."

Louisa moaned. "What will everyone think?"

"Don't you worry dearest, I'll defend your honor to the death," he comforted her. "However, let us hurry home and have Sally help you out of these clothes. We will just tell the truth to whoever asks, but pray no one will see us. Let us make haste sweetheart. I hope you will forgive me this inconvenience. I'm entirely at fault."

She adored his gallantry and gave him a kiss on the cheek. "That is to thank you again for the fan and your chivalry." She smiled, "And thank you so much for bringing Sally to me."

"She has told me how pleased she is to be working for you now. She never liked attending my aunt, God rest her soul. Nevertheless, three good things came because of her death. One is that my aunt no longer suffers. Another is that we are able to keep Sally on; she's been with the family since she was born to the housekeeper twenty-five years ago. Lastly, though I've told no one, except your father, I am the sole heir to the Tristam fortune."

Louisa's eyes opened wide, "Really David, what about your cousin Mr. Twackham?"

"The living is his wife's, as his mother, my aunt, was my father's youngest sister and she had only seven hundred a year." He smiled, "You my darling will soon be married to someone who has twenty times that amount. But we shall hear no more about that. Just suffice it to say that you'll never want for anything. Now shall we hurry home?"

It had been a long time since the Stuart sisters simultaneously thronged into one bedroom at Hedgerow. "Imagine Colette," Veronica said, "if you had not fallen in love with Basil, or that I had never become acquainted with Gavin."

"Had it not been so," Louisa sighed, "Mr. Tristam and I would not have met. Now if I forget to say, it means a lot to me that you're here tonight. I don't think I could have managed it alone. I want heavy eyelids when my head meets the pillow, or I shall not sleep a wink for the excitement."

"Just look at the four of you," Gabriella smiled.

Louisa patted Gabriella on the arm. "Don't worry dear sister, you are still young and there is yet hope. You are looking very well."

"Indeed," Veronica said, "I'm so proud of you. You've regained your youthful figure, and your lovely blond curls have recaptured their natural luster."

"Though you don't look like Louisa," Harriet said, "you are very pretty in your own right. But most importantly, I am pleased to see that you have become your true vivacious self with a bit of maturity added."

Veronica laughed, "Clearly you are no longer the silly and irresponsible sister we once knew."

"Do not pay heed to my misfortune, dear sisters," Gabriella smiled. "But know I'm gratified that each of you has found such a wonderful husband. And I believe you Veronica; I will find true love again, I am convinced of it."

"Good for you Gabriella." Colette laughed, "Just think, Veronica, how horrid it would have been had you married that Geoffrey Haydn, the young man from the other side of town. Things turned out rather sour for him, what with his father's ruination and them without a farthing. It was fortunate indeed that a relative from America paid for their passage to go and live there. I felt very sorry for your friend and his family."

"I did as well, the poor boy," Veronica declared as she brushed her hair. "But good came from it because I cannot imagine being without Gavin, and when I think of how close I came to marrying Mr. Haydn, it frightens me. Now Louisa, enough about me, we are here for you and it goes without saying that you have done eminently well for yourself. Nevertheless, you know it is not the money that will make you happy; it's your relationship with Mr. Tristam that will bring contentment. I should love and cherish Mr. Hunter with out his riches, for he is very dear to me."

"Indeed, look at me," Harriet chimed in. "Mr. Boswell and I have a small living and find joy in almost everything. Then there is Miss Phoebe with all that money and rarely a smile."

Louisa giggled. "David tells me that Miss Phoebe, with her fifty thousand, is desperate to have the Admiral propose and is quite unhappy that he has not. Yet, I dare say I doubt he would be foolish enough to waste his time with her if his intentions were not honorable. But I do not want to talk about money dear sisters; I am in hopes that you each might share some secret of how to put me at ease on the eve of my wedding day."

"Clearly we cannot spoil our evening talking about such affairs as poor Colette's unfortunate relations," Veronica laughed. "Now Louisa, I just want to give you some sisterly advise if I may and say that the excitement you feel now whenever you are with Mr. Tristam will turn into a deeper love and affection, one you cannot yet imagine. Your exhilaration is natural, though I think many a wife has never had the opportunity to experience it; alas they marry for the money only."

"Really, she is right Louisa," Harriet said. "Though it has been six months since our wedding, the butterflies in my stomach are still in a flutter whenever Mr. Boswell and I are together."

Gabriella laughed and asked, "Really Harriet, you mean to say that the Vicar's embrace thrills you? Please tell us more."

Harriet thought for a minute as she wrapped a loose strand of hair behind her ear. "Well I don't plan to divulge all my secrets, but here is one I will share with you. No matter how much Mr. Boswell begs me to be immodest, I always undress in private. I have often read that if the sizzle and intrigue leave a marriage then the romance will soon follow," she said proudly.

Louisa sighed as her cheeks colored. "What do you do after you are dressed for bed Harriet?"

"I'll show you." Harriet giggled, and then she stood up on Louisa's bed, where she unabashedly pulled her long nightgown up to her knees and began dancing.

"We'll have none of that here Harriet. Really I am shocked," Colette declared half serious, half amused, but Gabriella laughed and cheered her on to do more.

They were highly entertained picturing their straight-laced sister in such a scene, but Colette admonished them with, "Girls, this is a bride here asking for sisterly advice. It would not do to have the groom believe he married a hussy. If she comes to him appearing to know the secrets of a married woman, he will surely wonder."

"You are quite right Colette, though Harriet you must not think your advice is unwelcome," Louisa told her. "I appreciate it."

Harriet looked surprised and in all seriousness said, "Thank you for that. I was only trying to be helpful, because I know my John, and if he likes it why shouldn't Mr. Tristam?"

"Thank you Harriet," Louisa laughed, "I'll remember your counsel, but I have a question. Is dancing on the bed wrong?"

Veronica spoke up, "How is love to flourish if one cannot find happiness in intimacy! However, I think Colette is right; you would not want to dance like that in front of your husband on your first night together. He might wonder where you learned such a thing. Perhaps you should wait until you know each other a little better."

"I suppose you're right," Louisa sighed. "So then Veronica, would you tell us what Mr. Hunter asks of you?"

"Do not expect me to give away all my secrets," Veronica laughed, "I will not. One thing I will tell you is that Gavin likes to brush my hair before we go to bed; of course Margaret brushes it first before I join him in our bedroom. He loves running his fingers through like a comb. It is very romantic and a gentle way to proclaim his intentions.

On our honeymoon night, it certainly set me at ease; it still does.

"Oh Veronica that sounds so dreamy," Gabriella mused, wishing she had some romance in her life.

"Decidedly, it does," Louisa smiled. "Your sharing this is appreciated Veronica."

Veronica sighed, thinking how romantic Gavin could be. "It's a very private time for both of us."

"You have encouraged me," Colette said. "Now I will tell you of a particular thing about my Basil. And I shall never forgive any of you if I hear it repeated outside this room," Colette cautioned, and her sisters were all ears. "Basil loves to rub my feet."

They sat silent for a moment waiting for Colette to say more, and then Gabriella started to laugh. "Is that all? That is too funny. Truly, I don't see anything romantic in that."

Colette looked a little embarrassed but soon began to giggle with the others. "Well, I suppose one has to be involved to appreciate such tenderness. But now perhaps this news will appease you. Basil and I are expecting our second child in May. We are so pleased."

Her news was met with great joy and set off a discussion about having babies. Several hours later the sisters had divulged more secrets than they ever dreamed they would. To each of them any account of the mysteries of one's wedding night was of great interest, as was the subject of child bearing. Before they said goodnight, they vowed that what had passed from their lips would never go any further.

"Clearly things we've spoken of here only sisters could share," Veronica said. "And certainly I need not remind any of us that it would be positively indecent to mention a word of our secrets outside these bedroom doors."

As they got ready to say goodnight they all stood up and hugged each other and agreed never to say a word about their conversation. Prior to coming downstairs for breakfast the next morning, Louisa slipped Harriet and Gabriella each a fifty pound note. Additionally, before she sat down at the table she put the same amount of money into her mother's pocket; to her father she gave a hundred pounds.

The new young Pastor Witherspoon, engaged to Louisa's neighbor Sarah Grace Gerard, would preside over the wedding. Friends and family of David and Louisa anxiously waited for her in the Hedgerow Chapel that was filled with seven dozen potted gardenias flowering out of season. David wanted to surprise his bride, knowing that the gardenia was her favorite flower. He had never told her that he owned orangeries, where they grew oranges in the winter, as well as several flower houses filled year round with gardenias and roses.

Breathtakingly beautiful in her exquisite white satin gown covered over with pink silk lace, Louisa entered the chapel to musicians playing Mozart's Romanze Andante, another surprise from David. The beauty and fragrance of the gardenias along with the music took her breath away as she walked down the isle. Her dark hair, done high atop her head, held a diamond tiara with rubies and emeralds. It had belonged to David's mother. Louisa's cheeks glistened with tears as she moved towards him, and her beauty filled him with indescribable joy.

After the ceremony, the bride and groom walked out of the church to "Solomon", music from Handel's Queen of Sheba. Awaiting them sat a new burgundy barouche, trimmed in gold. David had it custom-crafted with his family crest emblazoned on the door. Two footmen held the door for them and two coachmen waited patiently to spur their six white horses on to the honeymoon destination. The carriage top had been removed so they could enjoy the perfect sunny day, and inside the coach, the creamy white satin cushions and leather floor were covered with gardenia petals.

"Oh David," Louisa said as the tears once again streamed down her cheeks. "It is so beautiful, the flowers, the carriage, everything. I love you so much." She stared at her surroundings, entranced by her fairy tale romance and her love for him.

"Come now darling," he said as he put his arm around her, "wave to your family and friends. You won't be seeing them again until twelfth night."

"Will you tell me now where we're going, or do I still have to be surprised?"

"Please be patient my darling and allow me to surprise you."

After waving goodbye for several minutes, they kissed passionately as they disappeared down the road. Their first stop before London was at the Morningside Inn, where they planned to spend ten glorious days before moving on to their luxurious London dwelling. They would spend a month there before going to Ivywood for the holiday festivities. In the spring David planned for them to travel to Paris and then sail the Mediterranean to Egypt for a trip up the Nile. After seeing the Nile, their final port before returning home was Bombay, India. Their entire honeymoon would last a full year.

Chapter 22

Snow covered the ground, and the fireplaces in Ivywood mansion burned brightly Christmas Eve. It was the coldest night anyone had seen in a long while. The twins, bundled in their nightclothes, were shown off to their family and friends gathered for the holidays. Louisa and David had arrived the day before and seemed quite content with each other. They had been away on the first part of their honeymoon for the past seven weeks.

As the Stuart sisters and their guests sang and played the pianoforte for everyone, David Tristam enjoyed watching Louisa chat with her sisters. He loved her simple happiness and the manner with which she was so easily pleased. She was agreeable to almost everything, yet she also spoke her mind when she felt strongly about something such as how their palatial London residence should be run. This show of intelligence was just one of many things David loved about his bride.

He knew that she was not wholly comfortable with some of his friends, who she said seemed to be rather haughty. Howbeit, David had been bored with their superficial lifestyle for years. Therefore, when he had to spend time with them he liked showing Louisa off, as in her quietness and simplicity they thought she might be dull. His greatest joy came in having her sing for them, and when they heard her, they thought her most charming and talented, and he became envied. Unmistakably she was beauty and innocence, a combination his friends had long forgotten existed.

As the ladies took turns at the grand piano singing and occasionally playing duets, Louisa sang a Christmas song that Gabriella had written.

My Lord, My God, the Son of Man, a child tonight will be. We wait and watch and see His light, for it shall shine from thee. Oh thank you Lord for giving us joy and peace divine. For My Dear God, we love you so and shall ever more be thine.

"That is a delightful song," Edward Ramsay said to Gabriella after Louisa had sung it twice over. "Am I to understand that you wrote both the lyrics and the music?"

"I did. I'm pleased you enjoyed it sir," she said, feeling privileged to be complimented by him.

Edward had never paid much attention one way or another to Gabriella. However, after seeing that she had some talent, he made a mental note to observe her more closely. *She is quite pretty*, he thought, as he looked around; *indeed, all the Stuart women are exceedingly favored.* As he sat there thinking about Gabriella's song, he heard a noise coming from outside. He went over to the window that faced the entrance to the mansion and peered out.

"Gavin," he motioned to him. "Come and have a look. Something is going on down there. I think we should see what's happening."

Immediately the two dashed outside with Basil and David following. Admiral Weatherby and John Boswell were close behind, as were Veronica, Louisa and Harriet. Before their very eyes they saw a knife wielding man chasing after a woman, who appeared to be dragging a small child while clutching another to her breast. Despite the cold, the moon shined brightly and illuminated the scene. Two servants dove toward the raging man and tried to grab him by the ankles; he tripped and fell but got away. Disoriented, he proceeded to run in the opposite direction of the woman and into the path of two runaway horses, which were harnessed together. Unable to escape their hooves the man was trampled to death. Edward Ramsay, the Admiral and John Boswell hurried over to him, while Gavin and Veronica bent over the young woman who had dropped to the ground. Harriet and Louisa took the howling children from her.

The mother related in shallow breaths what had happened. "My husband and I were headed for Liverpool to stay with friends. We planned to leave for America after the New Year." She gasped for air. "Our carriage lost a wheel and then tipped over on the road just outside your gates. My husband must have hit his head because suddenly he was as a wild man. The carriage had landed on me and I heard him screaming that he couldn't find his knife.

"The children did not seem to be hurt, but I could tell I was injured." She moaned and held her stomach. "I saw your lights in the distance. As soon as I managed to get out from under the coach, I grabbed the babies and started to run as fast as I could to get away from the Mr."

"Run and fetch the doctor," Gavin ordered one of the servants standing by. "Be quick about it man."

"I could see that he was of a mind to kill me," she breathed heavily. "Our money is in the buntings. Please I beg you," her voice pleaded. "The children are dear ones, they have nobody. There's no family only the father and I. Take care of my children; I beg you."

"What are the children's names?" Veronica asked through her tears.

The young woman in her last breath answered, "Allison—is two months, Robert is thirteen—" Suddenly the pain left her eyes and fear was replaced by peacefulness.

While in his quandary of what to do Gavin saw that the mother was dead. John Boswell came over and closed her eyes. Two servants carried her to a waiting area by the back of the kitchen; two others followed with the dead husband.

"Gavin," Veronica said anxiously, "We must make sure that the unfortunate babes are taken care of for the night."

"Of course," he answered, deep in thought, "Certainly, you're right."

It was highly unusual to take unknown children into one's private home rather than leave them to the servants care. Gavin had visited an orphanage once and was appalled by what he saw. The orphans there had looked frightfully unkempt as well as very sad, and the deplorable condition of the entire establishment held no joy. He did not intend to turn these babies out tonight or any night if he didn't have to.

Later that evening Veronica and he went to the nursery, and after kissing their curly headed, blond twins good night they looked in on the orphans. Little Robert had a full head of dark wavy hair and a happy face. Baby Allison, by her sweet smile, slept contentedly. Both children, now bathed and dressed in clean gowns, seemed so helpless and precious. They melted the hearts of their protectors as Gavin picked up Robert, and Veronica held Allison. Husband and wife took one look at each other and knew right away what they would do. Veronica gave instructions for the nursery.

"Miss Martin," she said, "Robert and Allison, are to be attended the same as you do Paul and Edward. You are to inform us if anyone disagrees with this, is that understood?" Veronica looked around the room and noticed that all but one of the nursemaids nodded their agreement. "And I want all the children dressed in fresh clothing and brought downstairs tomorrow morning."

As Veronica and Gavin left the room, she saw the servant who had looked disapprovingly raise her eyebrow to another nursemaid. "Impertinent," Veronica said to Gavin.

"What's that my dear?" he asked.

"It would appear that one of the nursery staff may not feel up to the task of treating the newcomers equally," she said explaining what she saw.

"Indeed," he replied. "All the servants will concur with our wishes or be dismissed. In the meantime tomorrow morning we'll have a look at the carriage and it's contents and see if we can't find something that will tell us a little more about Robert and Allison."

"I hope there is no lost relative or rich aunt longing for their presence," Veronica sighed. "After all we know nothing of them even though the mother said they had no one. We must be certain. They are so precious and lost now."

"They are indeed," Gavin smiled. "But first there must be a thorough investigation as you said, before we can even consider what I know you are thinking."

"Well, I believe you know me too well darling. However, let me just say that if we do take them in, we must raise them absolutely as our own. There can be no distinction, or I will not have them. Yet the thought of taking them to a home is dreadful."

"I agree," Gavin said. "It is imperative that we, as well as the servants, do not differentiate between Paul and Edward and the orphans for as long as they are here."

"I will not have it otherwise," Veronica replied.

Very early the next morning, Veronica crept out of bed while Gavin slept. She curled up on her pink velvet chaise in her boudoir and contemplated the events of the day before. *The idea of having two more children at Ivywood to bring up as our own is wonderful,* Veronica thought. *Clearly turning them out into the cold cruel world is inconceivable.* She wrapped her soft, warm blanket tighter around her leg and remembered the two little boys in Amiens. *I am occasionally haunted by them, though at the time I did not see that anything more could have been done. It saddens me to think of them, but now is perhaps the perfect opportunity to make up for that, at least a little.*

Chapter 23

For his Christmas gift to Phoebe Vance, Admiral Weatherby had placed an engagement ring in a tiny, jeweled sachet pouch and then put the pouch in a large, decorative box. In his conventional way he said little when she opened it. Even so, it was apparent to all by his unflappable smile, as he watched her put the ring on and swoon with joy, that he was pleased with himself. Mrs. Twackham waddled over to give her sister a kiss, and Basil followed to wish her and the Admiral well. Everyone else nodded their approval. Before they adjourned to the dining room, only one gift was left unopened.

"Gavin," Basil said, "before you show us Veronica's surprise, might you give us a brief understanding of why you have a large pine tree in this room?"

"Yes, of course. You see, as a child my father once visited an uncle in Dover around this time of year. He was astonished to find in his uncle's ballroom a tree such as this. The uncle explained that his German wife, who had grown up with a pine tree in her home every year to celebrate the birth of Christ, had insisted that he allow their children to enjoy the same tradition. In honor of our first Christmas together, Veronica and I decided it would be a wonderful thing to introduce into our celebrations."

"How unusual," Basil said. "I like the idea, though I know most people make more out of the New Year than they do Christmas, especially since it was banned during Cromwell's rule in 1652. I'm glad it was only eight years later that King Charles II reestablished the celebration, mild though it still is. I think I shall have a pine tree next year." Basil looked at Colette, "What do you think my dear, isn't that a fine idea?"

"Yes and it would be great fun to put some red ribbons on it to add more color." Colette smiled, "I like the idea very much."

"That sounds delightful, Colette. Perhaps next year we will try the same. "Now," Veronica laughed, "I cannot bear waiting a moment longer to uncover the surprise."

"All right darling, it is time for your mysterious package to be unveiled." Gavin reached for her hand.

"I must admit, ever since we entered this room I have wanted to peak under that immense piece of white cloth to see what is hiding under it."

"In just a minute you shall know." Gavin motioned for the servants to take the drape off. "I am as anxious to show you as you are to see it."

Behind the fifteen foot high Christmas tree two servants pushed a movable platform into the open and uncovered a magnificent sculpture. "This is for you darling," Gavin beamed, proud of his gift. "I saw you admiring it when we were in Rome and was reminded of our dancing the waltz together in Vienna. I found this to be the perfect reminder of our travels." As he walked with her to the statue, he whispered something in her ear, and she smiled, stifling a giggle.

Her smile pleased Gavin, as she and the others gaped at the larger than life size alabaster figures. "It is seven feet wide and ten feet high," Gavin expounded, running his fingers over the smooth stone; the brilliant masterpiece was of a woman in a long billowing gown dancing in the arms of an angel often mistaken for Cupid.

"It's exquisite," Veronica said sweeping her eyes up and down the giant sculpture.

Veronica looked closely at the detail. "It is magnificent and very reminiscent of our honeymoon. The couple blends so elegantly into one with the cloud beneath them. Thank you, I think we should keep it in here."

"I agree. I'm truly gratified that you like it so much," he replied, thinking, *the cost, coupled with the enormous amount of time and effort it took to transport it to Ivywood has made it all worthwhile just by the look on Veronica's face.*

"Shall we adjourn for breakfast?" he said as he took her arm; it was the Hunter tradition to give each other a gift on Christmas morning before eating.

Towards the end of their meal, Veronica sent word to Miss Martin to have the children brought to the dining room. Colette and Basil agreed that baby Charles should join them as well. He was a good-tempered nine-month old, whom everyone loved because of his contagious smile and precocious behavior. And now that Miss Phoebe wore a ring on her finger, she showed a little more interest in her nephew than before. Even the Admiral wanted to fuss over his soon-to-be nephew. He encouraged Baby Charles, who was having fun with the silverware, to make as much noise as he wanted.

"Oh you want to play with Uncle Thomas' nose, do you?" Weatherby laughed. "I grant you it is quite sizable for a nose. Treat it gently though," the Admiral winced, as the nursemaid attempted to take the child away. "No, no, leave him be. Tweak away my boy, you can't hurt this nose," he said, bearing a big grin, which exposed his teeth and made Charles giggle.

Somehow as everyone watched and laughed, the baby managed to wiggle onto the table and crawl across to Edward Ramsay. On his way he knocked over the drinks, had his knees in the kippers, porridge on his face, and his hands were covered with butter and jam. Miss Martin and the nursemaids tried to get to the baby as quickly as they could, but Edward held his hand up to stop them.

"I have him, and I don't mind at all that he spilled water on me," he declared. "I've had worse than this, but never by such a pleasing child." Edward lifted him high in the air and laughed. "There now little fellow, if we can't have some fun on Christmas morning, when can we?"

Each time Charles was tossed in the air, he giggled with delight and wanted more. Of course Edward obliged and was having as much fun as the baby until the last time around; the child heaved milk all over his new friend as gasps and sighs came from everyone.

Gabriella, being closest to Edward, jumped up to offer her help, but as she did she went headlong over her chair and fell on her face. As the nursemaids reached Edward and a servant came over to help wipe up the mess, no one saw that Gabriella had fallen. Edward laughed uproariously and everyone followed suit, relieved to see he was not upset. It was then that he saw Gabriella holding on to the edge of the table trying to pull herself up.

"My dear lady, let me help you," he said, forgetting that he was soaked with vomit as he lifted her in his arms and set her in a nearby chair.

"It's just my ankle," she said wincing bravely, while a servant wiped vomit from her bodice. "I don't mean to be so much trouble."

"May I check to see if it's broken?" he asked with genuine concern. "I feel quite responsible for this. Here you were only trying to help, just because I was being foolish. Please forgive me." He felt her ankle and proclaimed, "It is not broken, thank goodness. We do however, need to make you comfortable and prop this foot up. Shall we take you to your room?"

"Oh no, please, I don't want to be upstairs alone. Perhaps we could go the music room? Forgive me for being such trouble and spoiling everyone's fun," she said hoping she did not sound as awkward as she felt.

"Why don't we all go there?" Veronica said. "Miss Martin do not trouble yourself about the commotion, and Edward thank you for being so gracious."

Without anyone noticing, Admiral Weatherby made his way over to Gabriella, scooped her into his arms and carried her to a settee where she could sit with her feet up. Veronica asked that the orphaned infants remain with them while the nursemaids took the twins who were sound asleep back to the nursery.

As they waited for Edward to change into fresh clothes, Gavin held little Robert. Until that moment the boy had not made a sound, but then suddenly he let out a howl and began to cry. Louisa tried to comfort him with David's help, but the child was not to be appeased. One of the nursemaids started to come and take him, but Veronica stopped her as she handed Allison to her mother and went over to Robert.

"Poor thing," Veronica smiled. "You must be wondering where your mother is. Louisa, would you and Harriet like to play some Christmas music for us; that might soothe the baby's nerves."

A few minutes after the music started, Robert's cry became a whimper. Finally a little smile emerged as he pointed to the piano; a short time later he fell asleep. Miss Martin had him taken upstairs, but Veronica wanted Allison to stay a little longer.

Veronica held her with Gavin looking over her shoulder. "She is perfect isn't she?" he said, astonished at how precious and helpless she was. "I can see that to love her and her brother is as easy as loving Paul and Edward. May I hold her?"

Edward came down in fresh clothes and went right to Gabriella. "How are you feeling, Mrs. Newton?"

Amazed by his regard for her, she replied shyly, "I'm fine thank you, though perhaps a little tired."

Later that evening, Edward offered to carry Gabriella to the carriage so she could attend the Christmas night service at the church. "You must allow me to be of assistance Mrs. Newton. After all, it's entirely my fault that you are unable to get around."

"Sir, as much as I appreciate your kindness—" she tried to protest.

He held up his hand to stop her. "I must insist, unless you are feeling unwell, that you allow me to help."

"But that means you have to carry me in and out and all around," she objected. "I feel so silly."

"Please allow me the opportunity to make amends for my own

absurdity. It would be an honor for me to carry you this evening. I will be quite miserable knowing you are left behind because of me."

"Thank you Mr. Ramsay. As long as you are implacable in the matter, I see I have no choice." Even though her ankle was swollen and sore, his attention helped take her mind off it.

Just before Harriet and John left Ivywood to prepare for the Christmas evening service, they announced they were going to have a child in June, two months after Colette and Basil's second was due. When the Stuarts heard this they could not have been more thrilled; as far as they were concerned they could never have too many grandchildren.

Ivywood's chapel seated two-hundred and every seat was taken for the evening service. In addition to the exquisite stained glass windows, the congregation greatly admired the bench style seats covered with red velvet pads. This was a highly unusual feature, but Gavin's father had insisted upon it. From the pulpit John Boswell delivered his Christmas Night Sermon in the deep resonant voice he used when preaching God's word. It kept his audience very much awake on Sundays, as well as during special services like this evening.

"And I say to you my fellow men and women; we are made in the image of the only living God. We have been given freely, a Savior born this day, so that we may choose to lead lives, which directly reflect the love we have for God. He does not demand it of us, but rather makes it our choice.

"For whom among us would love on demand, but rather because we are loved, we choose to love in return. We are all, by birth, naturally hardhearted and sinful. Our willful natures cause us to think and do things that are unkind, unclean and unworthy of the love God has bestowed on us by sending Himself incarnate as the Son, Jesus Christ.

"His Son came to save us and forgive us our sins, but only by faith and accepting his sacrifice can we have salvation. Indeed, only through being saved from eternal hell fire and damnation can we truly love one another as God loves us."

Gavin loved to hear John Boswell preach, he knew that he was a true man of God. Like his father, Gavin was adamant about their

181

parson being able to live and breathe the Word from the Bible; he could not be timid in saying things the congregation might not like to hear.

"I will not have some insincere vicar who fears the opinions of men more than the will of God," Gavin had told Veronica when she first heard John preach. "My father always maintained that our vicar's kindness and way of life must reflect compassion and love for those he serves."

After the service Edward carried Gabriella back to the carriage. She was small and light and he liked being her conveyance. Additionally in his recent assessment of her, she seemed to be quite favorable in disposition. As for her pretty face, he found himself thinking often about the gentleness that exuded from her soft blue eyes, yet they carried a little sadness in them as well. Too, when they had parlor danced he remembered thinking that she was rather light on her feet, though the top of her head reached only to his chest. He wondered that he had not seen her beauty and countenance before now, but he reckoned his lubricity for Sarah Grace Gerard had distracted him.

"Mrs. Newton," Edward said, "I believe I have already told you how much I enjoyed your Christmas song."

"I am pleased you find my simple music so pleasant. And now I want to thank you with all my heart for your help today," she shivered as she spoke. "And if I may ask for just one last favor, it would be for you to take me directly to my room as soon as we return to Ivywood."

"Of course, I had planned to." Edward said, his smile turning to a frown. "But my, I have to say that you suddenly look quite pale. Perhaps insisting that you attend us this evening was a mistake."

"Not at all," her voice wavered, as she felt her forehead. "I did so want to come, though now I fear I may have a slight fever."

"We will get you to your room immediately, Mrs. Newton."

Gabriella tried to maintain that she would be fine, but as she protested, the pain in her eyes showed, and she fell unconscious upon Edward's shoulder. When the coachman opened the door, everyone agreed that the doctor should be sent for.

"She should never have been allowed out in the cold," the doctor admonished as Gabriella fever had climbed. "Her swollen ankle lowered her resistance, and that explains why she is ill. I have given her laudanum and that will see her through the night. However, someone should watch over her and keep compresses on her forehead to help keep the fever down. I shall return in the morning, and by then we may hope that she has improved."

Her mother was beside herself. "Oh my how could we have been so foolish? I will tend to her through the night," she said as she waved her daughters from the room. "One of you can relieve me in the morning."

When Edward Ramsay heard what the doctor had to say he insisted on sitting outside her door until the doctor returned. "I will make myself available should we need to fetch him before daylight," Edward said.

"How kind of you, it will be comforting to know that you are close by," Mrs. Stuart declared, thrilled by his offer.

"We shall pray for her safe keeping and a speedy recovery," Veronica said as she and Colette left the room. "Thank you Edward and mother, if you need anything please don't hesitate to send a servant for me."

In the morning, Gabriella seemed much improved. Her mother, who had also slept rather well beside her daughter, could not wait to inform her of Edward's attentions. "And you know," she exclaimed, "he resolved to spend the night outside your door in case we needed to call on the doctor before morning."

"I trust you will inform him right away that I am grateful indeed for his thoughtfulness. Tell him please," Gabriella said, her heart so full of joy at his selflessness that she was afraid she would burst into tears. "Tell him that I am much better now."

"I will do that," her mother smiled. "But the doctor said you should remain in bed all day. After all we want you well for the Bradford party the day after tomorrow."

"I don't plan to go anywhere today mother, and thank you for staying through the night with me."

Later on that afternoon there was a knock on Gabriella's door. "Would you see who that is please?" Gabriella asked Louisa, who had been visiting with her.

Louisa stepped out into the hall and returned with a grin. "It's Mr. Ramsay. He asked how you are and I told him you were doing well, but that he would have to come back in a half hour to see."

"Why ever did you do such a thing? You know I wanted to thank him for his kindness."

"Indeed, I did," Louisa laughed. "But look at you; we need to do something with that hair of yours and you must drape your pink velvet robe over you."

Gabriella gasped, "Oh sister, what would I do without you. I would have been mortified to have him see me like this. Thank you, now if you would call for my maid, I'd be grateful." Gabriella laughed, "Do you think a half hour is enough time to improve me?"

"Probably not, perhaps I should have Mr. Ramsay come back tomorrow," Louisa teased.

When Edward returned, Gabriella's maidservant let him in and then excused herself.

"I hear you are much improved Mrs. Newton," Edward smiled handsomely at her. "I am pleased to hear it."

"I want to thank you sir for your kind attention last evening and throughout the night. I trust you are rested."

"Yes, I am thank you. It grieved me entirely to see you feeling so poorly yesterday. Can you ever forgive me?" he sighed. "I should have known better."

"Why do you look so downhearted Mr. Ramsay?"

"I have ruined your chance of dancing at the New Year's Eve Ball. I feel I must make it up to you somehow."

"Mr. Ramsay," Gabriella replied, "Please do not fret so over me. I will be fine, my clumsiness was entirely my own fault; I should have been more careful."

Edward replied, "But if I hadn't insisted that you ride in the carriage to church in such freezing weather, you would not be lying here right now."

"Neither would I be dancing," she objected, "because I would still have twisted my ankle. There will be other balls, I dare say," she smiled feeling great contentment.

"Well, I will never forgive myself." Edward rubbed his chin as if thinking hard. "I hope that for the Bradford party you are well and that I may once again be your conveyance, as I am certain you will need one. Now I have a surprise for you." He reached around the outside of her door and pulled in a crutch that he had purchased in Broomfield from a man whose son no longer had need of it.

"Mind you now, Mrs. Newton, this does not mean that I will not be at your service. I assure you I will be by your side with almost every step."

"Mr. Ramsay, you are too kind. I think this will be most helpful. Thank you very much. And it will still be my pleasure to have you escort me to the party sir." Gabriella smiled sweetly.

They conversed further until supper was ready, and then she insisted on trying out her new crutch, despite having promised to stay in bed. After her maid helped her dress and fixed her hair, Edward walked with Gabriella to the dining room; everyone was astonished to see her up and about, with a crutch no less.

Chapter 24

Two days before the New Year, guests at Ivywood gathered for supper and cards at the Bradford's. Douglas and Lillian had taken great care to ensure a beautifully appointed home. Their table was set most fashionably for thirty guests with a flurry of red roses in Venetian crystal bowls and vases. The new green and white Wedgwood china held an exquisite fare of Turkey stuffed with chestnuts, roast beef, small pork pies, a variety of vegetables and fresh fruit in season, bread and rolls, miniature mince meat tarts, plum pudding and scrumptious chocolate delights. Along with this came goblets of mulled cider and orange grog. These choices, illuminated by shimmering candlelight and the gently glowing fireplace, offered a feast most befitting the newlywed's first party.

Douglas was exceedingly proud of his new home, his lovely bride and the luxury her wealth afforded them. More importantly he knew that he loved Lillian, with or with out her fortune. This pleased him greatly, as too many friends of his married for the money only. Lillian too, was gratified knowing that her husband sincerely loved her.

He stood and raised his glass to welcome his guests to their first social gathering. "Thank you dear family and friends for attending us this evening, I would like to toast our first Twelfth Night festivities together. May there be many more."

As they dined Lillian noticed contentment in Edward's countenance. *I don't think I have ever seen him look so well*, she thought as she watched him talk with Gabriella.

"Gabriella, we're glad to see you feeling better this evening," Lillian said. "I'm so happy you could join us."

"I would not have missed it for the world," she replied smiling at Edward. "However, I must give credit to Mr. Ramsay for seeing to it that I arrived."

"She speaks too kindly of me. Nevertheless, I am glad Mrs. Newton is well and can be here tonight too. And to that I raise my glass." Edward stood up. "Here's to good health, fine family and friends. May the coming year be the best ever."

After dinner, the men adjourned to their smoking parlor, while Lillian guided the ladies to her newly decorated drawing room. "This has become my favorite room next to my personal boudoir," she said proudly. "Here we can sip our tea or brandy and have conversation that does not concern the men. Please, everyone have a seat wherever you choose."

Veronica swept her arms out, admiring the yellow paisley draperies that covered a large window. It overlooked a barren rose garden and a grove of oak trees masked with snow. "You've put this room together perfectly."

Lillian smiled, pleased with Veronica's praise. "Thank you, I can't wait until the roses bloom so that I can sit up here at my writing desk and admire them."

"It's wonderful," Audrey agreed. "I don't think I would do a single thing differently."

"I spent a great deal of time deciding how I wanted this to be and finally settled on yellow velvet for the settees and blue floral silks for the chaises to bring out the colors in the paisley window coverings."

"I dare say for living in the country," Phoebe said indifferently, "that the room does have a certain sophistication about it. Don't you agree sister?"

Audrey raised her voice in disgust as she jumped to her cousin's defense. "Really Miss Phoebe, we are not peasants here, though you speak as if we are. As for Lillian, she hails from one of the wealthiest families in England, and I refuse to allow her to take your insult. Her mother carries the Essex name, which was here long before your family made their meager fortune in trade."

"I only meant to compliment," Phoebe said curtly. "I did not mean to offend. Please accept my apologies."

"Indeed," her sister mimicked. "No offense was intended. It's a lovely room. I think I've never seen anything quite as beautiful."

"I accept your apologies ladies," Lillian said as graciously as possible and changed the subject. "Now after we freshen up and have settled our dinner, I hope everyone will be ready for cards."

After several games of whist, Gabriella began to feel very tired. "Edward," she said when they took some refreshment, "you made me promise to tell you when I was ready to leave. Well, I'm sorry indeed to ruin your evening so soon, but could I impose upon you to see me home?"

Edward had feared for her well being because of the cold night air and quickly sent a servant for their wraps and the carriage. "I would have been angry if you had not asked." He turned to the other guests and announced, "Mrs. Newton, being true to her word, has asked me to see her home. Is there anyone else who is ready to retire early? If so can we offer you a ride back to Ivywood?"

"I believe my wife is tired, if you don't mine we will take you up on your offer," David Tristam replied.

"Ah yes. David and Louisa, please join us." Edward said with just the slightest hint of disappointment that he could not ride alone with his charge; howbeit, only Mrs. Stuart detected the smallest change in his countenance. "Shall we go then, I believe the carriage is here?"

When they arrived back at Ivywood, Gabriella said good night to Edward and the Tristams. As soon as she went to bed, fatigue swept over her when her head dropped to the pillow, but rather than fall asleep right away as she had hoped to do, she found herself thinking about Edward.

I am astonished by his consistent desire to attend me. I believe he's done more than anyone could expect, and now he wants to collect me in the morning and help me down to breakfast. How I love his smile and his contagious laugher. Amidst her reflections she suddenly realized that she cared a great deal for him. Her last thought before she drifted off to sleep was of Edward carrying her up the stairs in his arms.

She woke up in the morning with a start. *What a horrid dream I had last night.* She laughed out loud, pushing her hair from her eyes. *Yet it was too silly to be true, I hope.*

Edward and she had gone horseback riding through Ivywood's grounds. They were wholly enjoying each other's company, when up from behind them came Miss Phoebe and Mrs. Twackham.

"Edward," Phoebe shouted. "You promised you would ride with me this morning. What are you doing with that woman? She has nothing to offer; you will do so much better with me as your wife." Phoebe snarled and her hair went flying out from under her ugly, black hat. "Away with you, you wench," she waved her hands at Gabriella to shoo her from her sight.

In her dream Edward had made no reply to Miss Phoebe's rude behavior, nor had he tried to stop Gabriella as she rode away. When she looked back to see if he might be following her, she saw that Miss Phoebe, despite her hideous hairdo, was enfolded in Edward's arms.

As Gabriella reviewed her dream, Judy, her maidservant, helped her dress. "Are you all right Mrs. Newton? You have a sadness about you that I have not seen in some time."

"Judy, I had the worst dream last night; a nightmare actually," she said and then proceeded to tell her about it.

Judy chuckled, "Now Mrs. Newton, you know that truly was a nightmare, but thank goodness that is all it was. Of course, I think Mr. Ramsay is much too smart to fall for the likes of that woman. You have no fears now my lady. All will be well, I am certain of it." Judy had spent the next hour doing Gabriella's hair and boudoir, all the while trying her best to convince her that Edward probably cared little for Miss Phoebe.

When Edward arrived at her door, he smiled broadly thinking, *I never cease to be pleased by Gabriella's shyness and beauty.* "You are looking very well this morning, Mrs. Newton. I trust you slept well and feel refreshed?"

His deep blue eyes studied her purple velvet gown, which showed off her smooth neck and attractive bosom. Her blond curls fell softly over her ears, and shapely pink lips beckoned him welcome, as did the twinkle in her eyes. These things he had noticed in her over the past few weeks, but never so much as he did this morning. The moment they were alone, he immediately sat in the chair next to Gabriella's bed and took her hand.

Gabriella looked surprised. "Mr. Ramsay," she said shyly, "is there something you wish to say? Perhaps it might be considered imprudent of me to allow you to sit so near when we're alone."

"We're not quite alone, Mrs. Newton. After all, the door is open."

"Yes," she laughed, "and we have plenty of cool air to keep us company. But forgive me, I did not mean to be rude. I see that you intend to be serious. I trust I haven't offended you."

"Dearest Gabriella," he said taking her hand in his. "My precious Gabriella," he paused and wiped his brow. "Forgive me; please permit me to be bold. You see," he stammered. "I, since, I mean, since you injured your ankle on my behalf and even before that, I cannot say exactly when, but—, you see I have fallen in love with you. Indeed my heart overflows with love for you. Will you consent to be my wife, for I should like very much to take care of you for the rest of your life?"

He kissed her hand and looked into her eyes; gazing back at him was a face full wonder. "Mr. Ramsay, I, I don't know what to say. This is unexpected. After all, for a person of such eminence and wealth as you, why would you want me for your wife?" Tears streamed down her cheeks, "I'm so unworthy of your notice, I lack fortune and connections, and I've made terrible mistakes in my life." She sobbed, covering her face with her tiny manicured hands. "Oh Edward, to hear you say you love me is very hard for me to believe, as I see no honor in this for you. Clearly, you are putting your reputation at risk by favoring me."

"Nonsense, you're not to worry about my reputation. I care nothing for the opinions of those who may disapprove, but if you do not love me that is another story." he frowned. "That is not it, is it? Please say that you will be my wife, I love you so very much."

"Oh Edward," she wiped her eyes, "I do love you, I do. I'm honored that you asked me marry you, but, but...."

"My love, you are wrong if you consider yourself unworthy. Everyone deserves happiness and that is how I feel when I am near you; there is no value in my wealth if I have no one to share it with. I want that someone to be you. Rank and fortune mean nothing to me; I want only your happiness and for you to love me as I do you."

She wiped her eyes. "I have admired you from the first time we met Edward, but all hope seemed beyond my reach. Though there are few even with pristine backgrounds that I feel would deserve such attentions from you. You are as wonderful and full of life as anyone I have ever met."

He put his arms around her and kissed her passionately. "Say you'll marry me my darling," he whispered in her ear, enjoying the delectable sensation of their embrace.

"I will marry you Edward," she said as he held her tight. "I love you and would be proud to be your wife if you're absolutely certain it's what you want." They kissed again, and she felt his love for her all the way down to her toes.

He sighed, breathing heavily, and then finally he held her by the shoulders and leaned back to look at her. "You are so beautiful Gabriella." He ran his hand his over her silky blond tresses and brushed them from her flushed cheeks.

She smiled broadly and touched his face, "Thank you. I cannot believe this is happening to me. I thought I should never know happiness again."

As they sat holding hands, talking, Gavin saw them and started to turn away. "Forgive me," he said, "I did not mean to intrude."

"Not at all, my dear cousin, come in, come in," Edward stood. "We have something to share with you, and I am honored that you will be the first to know." Edward looked at Gabriella. "Do you mind my love if we tell your brother-in-law before the others?"

"By all means, he should be the first to know."

Gavin listened and was pleased to see that his once unhappy sister-in-law had a smile on her face like that of a sunbeam. Edward too reveled in Gabriella's acceptance, and without another word he lifted her into his arms. The three of them went downstairs to the dining room, where the guests were beginning to go through the breakfast buffet.

Edward set Gabriella down on a chair and with grand eloquence proudly announced, "My dearest family and friends, Gabriella has consented to be my wife."

Mrs. Stuart ran to her daughter, expressing her elation with hugs and kisses; her sisters followed suit. At the same time Edward asked to speak to Mr. Stuart and apologized for not coming to him first. He was forgiven as Mr. Stuart gladly bestowed his consent.

"After all, Sir," he reminded Edward, "she is not a child. She is free to do as she wishes. However, I want you to know that I could not have chosen a better man to be her husband."

Amid all the excitement, Phoebe Vance glowered and whispered to her sister, "I am all amazement. What can he possibly see in her? She is so lacking in distinction, even more so than her twin, who had the nerve to marry our cousin. I am mortified."

"Now sister," Ursula Twackham said with her mouth full of bread, "you must remember your own happiness. You have the Admiral to think about now."

"You're quite right. However, I will never understand why esteemed gentlemen such as Mr. Ramsay or Mr. Hunter and especially Mr. Tristam, would want to marry country girls who are so unworthy of the honor."

"Tell me dear, have you decided on your own wedding date yet?"

"June seems to suits us both," Phoebe replied with a puckered brow, still brooding over Edward's news.

She finished breakfast in silence, with the Admiral ignoring her as he conversed jovially with Edward and Gabriella about their future together.

Chapter 25

There was a knock at the door as Veronica sat at her vanity. "Can I be of further assistance to you my lady?" Margaret asked. "If not, the Master is waiting for you in the other room. He asked me to tell you."

"Thank you Margaret, I think we are done for now, and I won't be changing again until the ball. Mr. Hunter and I are going to have a light supper brought up early this evening, and then I will rest and want you to help me dress at eight thirty. In the meantime, will you have coffee and scones sent to my private parlor in about a half hour please. My sisters and I are going to have some time together before we join the other guests downstairs."

"Of course my lady," she smiled and opened the door for Gavin.

"I'll be only a minute here," Gavin said, "but I thought you might want to know what I've learned from the investigator about the orphans."

"Of course, tell me please. I hope it is good news."

"It is too soon to know much, but he has spoken to the couple Robert and Allison's parents were planning to stay with before going on to America. They say they did not know the family well, only that the husbands were acquaintances from the bank where they worked together at one time. Apparently they are in no position to take the children, therefore, they will continue on here while the matter is looked into further. My man said he should have more information for us in about a month."

"A whole month, I shall be quite eager to know all. Thank you for coming to tell me, darling."

"I know you are about to have your sisters up for coffee, so I will see you later."

As Gavin was leaving Veronica's sisters came in, eager to know the reason why their oldest sister had asked them to gather together. "I thought it would be good for just the five of us to celebrate Gabriella's engagement," Veronica said greeting them with a smile. "I wanted us to talk before we join everyone in the parlor."

"I'm so glad you asked us Veronica," Gabriella twittered. "Next to being with Edward, being with my dear sisters is a very good thing."

"Have you and he talked much about your future together?" Louisa asked.

"Not yet, though he said he would like to discuss a wedding date and our honeymoon plans tonight while we watch the ball."

Veronica sat silent for a moment, studying her sisters. "Just look at each of you, I am so proud of you. But, aside from celebrating Gabriella's happiness with sweet cake, I wanted to speak with you about Robert and Allison."

"They are so precious," Louisa sighed.

Colette agreed and asked, "Do you think they will stay with you here at Ivywood?"

"We won't know anything until the inquiries on their behalf are complete. So far we've come up with very little, but clearly they are easy to love. We would like to adopt them if there is no other family to take them in. However, if we are able to keep them we wish for the children not to know they are adopted until they are of an age to understand. Even then we ask that you not speak of it outside this room. This is a matter of great concern to Gavin and me, and he is going to say something to the gentlemen about our wishes. We have already dismissed two servants for voicing their disapproval of our allowing the orphans in the same nursery with Paul and Edward. Others will also treat the children differently if they know they are not truly from the Hunter blood line."

"I am sure we agree," Colette said confidently. "And I speak for all of us dear sister."

Gabriella, Harriet and Louisa concurred, and for the next hour the five of them chatted and giggled like school girls about children, weddings and honeymoons and that evening's ball.

"Lord and Lady Gavin Hunter," the stout, dignified steward announced for all to hear. The handsome couple entered the room to the eyes of three hundred and fifty guests, who had waited anxiously for their arrival. Speculation had it that after a year and a half the Hunters still behaved like newlyweds. Veronica's beauty was as renowned as her husband's taste in clothes and jewels for her. Without a doubt they were well celebrated for their generosity and their unusual ideas.

With eloquence, distinguished looking Gavin welcomed their guests. "I would like to announce that it will be a tradition at each Ivywood Ball here after to begin and end with a waltz." He motioned for the orchestra to commence with a Mozart Waltz in three-quarter time.

The radiant pair did the honors of beginning the evening's first dance as they twirled past the magnificent marble sculpture, which their company had greatly esteemed beforehand. Veronica donned a new Paris gown of light-blue, satin with sapphires and lace at the revealing neckline. She seemed like one floating on a cloud with the marble sculpture and the gleaming white floor, as Gavin and she gracefully waltzed around the room.

"Darling, you are absolutely stunning tonight." Gavin smiled handsomely at her. "I am certain that I'm envied because of your beauty."

"You flatter me, my love, but I cannot say I'm offended. However,

I am quite sure that many of the ladies here resent me for having such a handsome and generous husband."

He chuckled and they danced and looked over at Gabriella and Edward. "Your sister and my cousin seem to be very content just watching everyone."

"I believe they are quite happy," Veronica replied. "I have not seen Gabriella in such high spirits for several years. I am glad for her, and your cousin."

A brocade settee had been brought in for Edward and Gabriella to sit on and observe the ball. "My darling Gabriella," he said as they viewed the dancers, "you have made me so happy. I want us to be married as soon as possible, and I'd like very much to take you to either Europe or America for our honeymoon. It will be your choice."

"I too am anxious to be married, and with as little fuss as possible. I was thinking May would be a good time. As to America or Europe, I hope you will allow me time to think about which one, or perhaps I will want you to choose. After all you have been to both places and I know nothing of either."

"We can think about that together then. But could not the wedding be sooner? Now that you have agreed to be my wife, it will be difficult to be patient. Nevertheless, I understand there are things to be done and if properly, I must curb my anticipation; indeed, you are worth the wait." He patted her hand and looked handsomely at her with a broad smile. "What would you say to the month of April? You and your mother and father can take up residence in London as my guests for the winter. I know of a very fine estate there that is available; it would suit all of us nicely. We could leave for our honeymoon as soon as the weather permits, and upon our return we will settle in at Lochaven. Please allow us to be bold and wait no longer than April."

Gabriella was too full of excitement to fall into a dispute of only a month. "April it shall be then."

"My dear I am so inspired, there is much to be done, and I will be glad for the occupation of preparing. I want you and your mother to do all the shopping you like, and you are to have the finest money can by."

Gabriella was ecstatic. "Spending the winter shopping in London would thrill me, and of course mother beyond her wildest dreams. She has often said how she would like to stay a couple of months in the city without a care in the world. Certainly Father will also consider a stay in the city, particularly with you, quite enjoyable. You are too generous Edward."

"I shall enjoy his company as well, and I am gratified that you and your mother will be pleased."

Edward had known many women over the past ten years, the majority of them he liked because they had great beauty, but he knew that most lacked character. He loved Gabriella because she did not take life for granted. His had been consumed with acquiring wealth, and although successful in that pursuit, he had never attained true personal happiness. *But for Gabriella, I might never have found it*, he thought, studying her as she admired the dancers.

"You know my love," he said putting his finger to her lips, "I love your heart shaped mouth and the way the corners turn up when you smile." He gazed at her as she brushed a wispy blond curl from her porcelain neck. He wanted to reach out and pull her into his arms.

"Oh Edward, how you go on," she said swooning inside, feeling like the most fortunate girl in all of England to have captured his heart.

"It is not flattery, it is the truth," he said with tenderness in his voice. "You know darling, I wish my mother could have known you. She would have been proud of my choice for you as my bride. You have her gentle spirit, and it would please her to see that I have finally found true love, the same love she had with my father."

"I am glad she would be pleased."

"Mother talked often about my father and his good character," Edward said. "She told me that he always used to say, 'Money my darling wife isn't everything. Never put your faith in it, but always in God alone. He will provide.' I never believed her until now. Indeed, I have always done just the opposite and with great enthusiasm, especially after mother died. I was bent on becoming richer than my wildest dreams, and I succeeded. In my search for riches and happiness I gravitated towards grasping, conceited women, or I settled for naive, young ladies. Finding you has been my greatest joy, for I know you truly love me."

"You were most dazzling tonight." Gavin said to Veronica, after the ball and all the guests had bid goodnight.

"Thank you," she sighed. "I wonder that I blush when you talk so. You know darling, my love for you grows deeper each day, and it has become something very beautiful." She spoke as she ran her ivory handled brush through her hair while sitting at her dressing table.

"Let me do that for you," he said taking the brush from her soft hand. As he smoothed her sable curls, he dreamily admired her amatory figure, which was silhouetted through her elegant pink satin gown and robe; he did not need the glow of the fire to keep him warm.

"Darling, our love for one another surpasses all I have ever thought possible," he whispered as he put his strong arm around her tiny waist. "Why don't we sit by the fire for a bit before we go to bed?"

He took her by the hand and led her to the plush, bearskin rug and pulled her down beside him. With a chair pillow under her head and him leaning on his elbow, they gazed at each other in silence then fell into a passionate embrace as the warm, white bear covering enveloped them.

Several hours later Veronica woke to the cold night air as the fire had nearly died out. She stared down at her sleeping husband. Moving his black wavy hair from his high forehead she kissed his firm, determined lips and whispered, "You are my true love."

He woke with a start and smiled up at her. "It is quite frosty in here, perhaps you will allow me to carry you to the cozy comfort of our down quilts and soft pillows," he said as he stretched and stood.

"I think I can get there quicker on my own." She jumped up giggling and dashed for their four poster bed.

He was right behind her. Unexpectedly he lifted her up by the waist and tossed her onto the satin coverlet. "You're right, you were quick, look at that you beat me." He laughed uproariously and hurried to get next to her. Soon they were both fast asleep enjoying the warmth of their bodies next to each other buried under the mound of feather and down comforters.

Printed in the United States
65801LVS00001B/76-135

9 781424 138166